I0689829

THE SPIDER:
JUDGEMENT OF THE DAMNED

# MASTER OF MEN!
# SPIDER®

# JUDGEMENT OF THE DAMNED

*By Grant Stockbridge*

POPULAR PUBLICATIONS • 2026

© 1940, 2026 Argosy Communications, Inc. All rights reserved.

THE SPIDER® is a trademark of Argosy Communications, Inc.
Authorized and produced under license.

PUBLISHING HISTORY

"Judgement of the Damned" originally appeared in the June, 1940 (Vol. 21, No. 1) issue of *The Spider* magazine. Copyright 2026 by Argosy Communications, Inc. All rights reserved.

ALL RIGHTS RESERVED

No part of this book may be reproduced or utilized in any form or by any means, electronic or mechanical, without permission in writing from the publisher.

This edition has been marked via subtle changes, so anyone who reprints from this collection is committing a violation of copyright.

Visit POPULARPUBLICATIONS.COM for more books like this.

# CHAPTER 1
## SUMMONS FROM HELL

IT WAS a regulation legal document in many respects, an injunction to stay Joseph Briscoe from operating the Frisco Club.

The writ was returnable at midnight "... under pain of the displeasure of Judge Torture." The word *pain* was underlined.

Another irregular aspect of the procedure was the suitcase which the unseen process server had left with the writ. The suitcase contained a man's leg. It had been mangled in one of the simpler torture devices used by the Spanish Inquisition... a gyve.

Richard Wentworth glanced from the paper to the ghastly contents of the suitcase. A white line of anger etched itself about his mobile lips. He looked up into the rigidly set face of Joseph Briscoe.

"You're a brave man, Briscoe," Wentworth said slowly. "Not many men, either within or outside the law, would have had the courage to ignore this... summons."

Briscoe poured himself a drink, sat down behind his desk and tossed off the liquor. His voice came out harshly. "Personally, I think I was a damned fool," he said. "I've been trying to go straight ever since you gave me my chance, Mr. Wentworth. And every shake-down artist in town has been pot-shotting at me. I'm not brave. I was just sore. I was plenty sore. Now... I don't know."

1

NEW YORK
MMONED TO APPEAR

Wentworth glanced at his wrist watch. "Quarter past two," he said. "This man who calls himself Judge Torture should know by now that you aren't going to submit to his muscling in on your club. You still refuse to call the police?"

Briscoe said, raspingly, "Don't make me laugh. The coppers? They won't believe I've gone straight! They keep dogging me!"

"They would protect you," Went-

3

worth said quietly. "The kind of man you have been, Briscoe, doesn't usually go straight... What are you going to do?"

Briscoe leaned forward to pour himself another drink. His face was bone-white and there was a glitter in his eyes.

"I'll tell you what I've done, Mr. Wentworth," he said spitting out his words. "I got the old gang back here again, and they won't wait until I'm dead to help me! But I wanted to tell you, Mr. Wentworth. I've tried! No man ever tried harder. The damned crooks, and the damned coppers, they won't let me! But I wanted to play fair with you, same as you played fair with me!"

Wentworth rose slowly and laid the paper on the desk. He glanced once more at the suitcase. His intelligent, well-bred face was utterly without expression. He was a powerfully compact man, with an easy confidence in the carriage of his shoulders, in the lift of his head. His evening dress was perfectly tailored.

Any man, and all women, would look at him more than once, even in a casual passage. There was a commanding aura that overlaid the quietness of the man... that labeled him instantly a leader, a Master of Men! But none had ever suspected that he lived another existence, a secret life of self-less service to mankind. He was the lone wolf of justice whom all the Underworld feared. He was... the Spider!

Briscoe, rigid with the fear of the defiance he had hurled, did not know that. He only knew that Wentworth had offered him a chance to go straight after his prison term, had even financed him in the club.

BRISCOE HELD his blunt-fingered hands across the desk. "Maybe I ought to have phoned you first, Mr. Wentworth," he said. "But me, I'm a man who's always stood on his own two feet. I'll take care of this Judge Torture! My boys will pump him full of lead."

Wentworth nodded quietly. "You don't know anything about this Judge Torture? Never heard of him before this paper and suitcase were delivered by express?"

"No, Mr. Wentworth," Briscoe said.

"And this address of Judge Torture's court?"

"There ain't no such place, Mr. Wentworth," Briscoe said. "This Judge Torture must have planned some sort of snatch. Let him come. I'm ready for him!"

He stiffened and his eyes widened horribly as they gazed into Wentworth's. He gasped, whipped about toward the window. It was closed, but the sound seemed to come from that direction. It was a cackling heinous laughter. And then… a voice spoke!

*"It is fortunate you are ready for me, Briscoe,"* it said. *"Very fortunate. For I, too, am ready for you!"*

Wentworth's voice was a crisp command. "Steady, Briscoe," he said. "That speech came over a microphone hook-up. There's nobody at the window. Instead…."

Wentworth spun toward the door, his right hand moving with blurred speed. A powerful automatic appeared in his fist. Even so, he was almost too late. Under the cover of that speech, a man had stepped inside the door!

The man was curiously dressed. He wore an ordinary business suit, but from his shoulders swung a doublet of the fashion of the sixteenth century. He carried no weapon in his hand save a tipstaff, a wand tipped with metal such as the bailiffs of old

English courts had carried in token of authority.

The man ignored the gun in Wentworth's fist, paid no attention when Joseph Briscoe strode around his desk and clawed out a revolver. He spoke in sonorous tones.

"Joseph Briscoe!" he intoned. "I summoned you to appear before Judge Torture, and you ignored that summons! I have come to arrest you for that failure, and all persons are hereby warned that any interference with the due performance of my duty will earn the displeasure... of Judge Torture!"

Wentworth's eyes were narrowed as he stared in amazement at the man. Briscoe had called the summons "a screwy kind of shakedown racket." It was scarcely an adequate description. This thing was incredible. Apparently, a criminal had set up a court with the intention of mulcting whomever he wished. But he had not been content with that mummery. He had even dressed his agent in the style of antique courts and armed him with a tipstaff!

It was macabre, a masquerade of law and order. It might have been ridiculous... except that on the floor beside the door was the suitcase with its ghastly memento of torture and slow, violent death!

Briscoe cried out in a strained, hoarse voice, and there was a solid thump on the floor.

Briscoe said thickly, "I—I couldn't hold my gun. It got—*hot!*"

## JUDGEMENT OF THE DAMNED

THE BAILIFF of Judge Torture permitted a wintry smile to cross his lips. "Joseph Briscoe," he said, "come with me!"

Briscoe cried out, "No, No, I won't come!"

Wentworth heard him take a step forward, and then another. They were laborious steps. He was fighting against them. He was shouting his protests… and still he walked toward the bailiff with the tipstaff, obeying while he insisted that he would not obey!

"This has gone far enough," Wentworth said shortly. *"Drop that tipstaff!"*

The bailiff swung his eyes toward Wentworth. His fist gripped the wand more resolutely, and its metal tip was pointed toward Briscoe. Apparently, that harmless looking wand of metal-tipped wood contained the power to drag Briscoe forward against his will! And it had heated the gun from Briscoe's hand!

"I have given the ritualistic warning," the bailiff said harshly. "Do not interfere… *under pain of Judge Torture's displeasure!"*

Wentworth did not smile. His lips scarcely moved for his words. "I will give you precisely two seconds to drop that tipstaff," he said flatly. *"One…."*

The bailiff's eyes flashed contempt… until they met the cold gaze of Wentworth! Then they flared wide in sudden shock! He had met in the gaze the bitter will of the Master of Men!

The bailiff cried out hoarsely. He wrenched the wand about and the metal tip caught a gleam of light. It was as if a fat spark leaped from its point!

Shock ran through Wentworth's right arm! His automatic

7

burned his palm with an incredible, searing heat! And suddenly all of Wentworth's muscles urged him forward!

Wentworth realized in that instant that he faced some new and tremendously powerful weapon of the Underworld... of Judge Torture! This tipstaff was not the innocent wand of wood and metal that it seemed. In some strange way, it could focus heat upon his gun... and it could compel his will! It could even compel the superb will of Richard Wentworth—the Spider!

Realization and action came in the same flashing instant. Wentworth dropped the gun. Instead of fighting against the pull of the wand, he used that powerful compulsion as a *jiu-jitsu* expert uses the attack of his opponent. He hurled himself upon the bailiff!

Wentworth's left fist struck savagely at the man's wrist. The wrist was rigid as iron, but it gave way under Dick's furious blow. There was a dull crack, as if a dry stick had been broken. The man cried out hoarsely. The wand flew from his grasp. Wentworth's right snapped toward the bailiff's jaw. Incredibly, the man evaded that punch. Wentworth's fist only grazed past the side of his head! The man drove his left solidly into Wentworth's *solar plexus!*

The force of the blow was doubled by the speed of Wentworth's leap to the assault. Wentworth's superb muscular development was the only thing that prevented a knockout. As it was, he spun aside from the blow. His heels came solidly down upon the floor as his hands flew up in defense.

But the bailiff did not press his advantage. He hurled himself past Wentworth and snatched Wentworth's automatic from the floor. Wentworth shouted as he drove forward. He kicked out with the shrewd skill of a *savate* expert. But even as his foot connected with the bailiff's gun wrist, the automatic spat its spear of flame! Wentworth felt the sear of the heat past his side, felt the bullet pluck his clothing. Behind him, there was a wheezing gasp from Joseph Briscoe. But Wentworth was upon the bailiff.

HIS OUTSTRETCHING hand seized the barrel of the automatic and he wrenched it free. With it, he struck a calculated force blow. He did not want to kill the bailiff—not until he could talk about his master. Judge Torture! One thing ruined his plan. The bailiff dived forward and the automatic slashed into the back of the man's head just where vertebra met skull!

The gun jarred from Wentworth's grip, skidded across the room. The bailiff sagged to the floor—dead!

Wentworth swore harshly, reeled to his feet.

On the floor lay the motionless body of Joseph Briscoe. Blood stained the stiff bosom of his dress shirt, but it no longer flowed from the wound over his heart. That one accidental shot had killed him instantaneously!

For an instant, Wentworth stood braced with strain. No sound of alarm penetrated the office. Of course. Briscoe had sound-proofed it against the ceaseless beat of the swing orchestra of his Frisco Club.

9

RICHARD WENTWORTH

Wentworth stared down at the motionless body of the bailiff. He stooped toward it and, with a sudden violence flipped it over on its back. The sightless eyes stared fixedly at the ceiling. Wentworth's face was grim and cold. Joseph Briscoe had been a criminal once, but with Wentworth's help, he had been fighting

the slow hard road back to honesty. He had been courageous…
and he was dead because of that bravery.

Wentworth's fingers slipped into his vest pocket. He thumbed
open the base of his cigarette lighter, stooped and ground the
base of the lighter against the flesh of the bailiff's forehead.
When Wentworth straightened, there gleamed on the cooling
flesh, a crimson seal of sprawling hairy legs and poison fangs—
*the seal of the Spider!*

And Wentworth stood with the glacial chill of his gray-blue
eyes implacable upon the dead man. Let Judge Torture beware!
The Spider gave warning only once!

So intent was Wentworth that he was unaware of what
occurred behind him, had not yet noticed that the window
was open now. Through that window a man's hand reached
cautiously to the floor, where lay Wentworth's automatic—the
gun that had killed Joseph Briscoe! That bore Wentworth's
fingerprints!

While Wentworth searched of the man's body, that hand
closed upon the gun. It lifted… and for an instant, that deadly
black muzzle centered upon Wentworth!

Through a space of heartbeats, the gun held like that, the finger tightening on the trigger!

While the unseen assassin hesitated, a curious thing happened. From the bailiff's wand, which had flown across the room under the impact of Wentworth's blow, came a sharp, muffled explosion!

Wentworth's eyes flicked to the wand, which had burst into hot, consuming flames! And the assassin's hand, still clutching the gun, vanished into the night!

Wentworth sprang toward the flaming tipstaff. A full pace away, he checked and flung up an arm before his face. The heat from that small blaze was incredible! Already, behind it, the plaster wall was cracking and powdering. Paint blistered on the floor and burst into flame. The rug was smoldering into fire!

WENTWORTH RETREATED a pace. Then he snatched a tapestry from the wall and flung it over the blaze. He plucked up a chair and ground it down upon the tapestry in an effort to smother it. For seconds longer, tongues of flame lanced up even through the tapestry... then they died. Wentworth removed the remnants of the tapestry and the chair. Of the wand, nothing at all remained!

He stood rigidly in the middle of the office, the stench of heat in his nostrils. It was incredible that, under his very eyes, a criminal could stage such a raid. But it had been done, and Wentworth had no clue at all.

Only a suitcase with a severed human leg, and an address given in a legal paper... an address that did not exist!

While Wentworth stood there, his mind ranging over the

menace incorporated in this strange criminal who called himself Judge Torture, a new sound smote upon his ears. He heard it, far off and faint, but unmistakable!

The whine of police sirens!

He was in action instantly. He could not afford to be found here, where the seal marked the Spider's kill. He had, as Wentworth, warm admirers among the police. The Commissioner, Stanley Kirkpatrick, was his closest friend. But the police could not be swerved from the stern prosecution of the Spider!

Wentworth bounded first toward the window. Even in the turmoil of action, he knew which way his gun had been hurled. Too often, his life as the Spider had depended upon recording a fact, even in the midst of battle. His eyes went to the spot beneath the window where he knew the gun should rest—and it was only then he saw that the window itself was now open!

Instantly, he knew that the gun had been removed in that way. He leaped to the window. From the darkness of the alleyway below him, a gun sent its lance of flame toward him!

Wentworth ducked and the glass tinkled with a faint musical mockery. His lips twisted in a faint smile. Judge Torture planned well!

Three long strides took Wentworth across the room. He used a handkerchief to wipe the doorknob clean. He gripped the knob with it, twisted... The knob would not turn! The door was locked from the outside!

Wentworth whirled to stare toward the smashed window; the darkness out there harbored more enemies. On the floor lay the dead bailiff, with the mocking seal of the Spider on his forehead... certain death if Wentworth were caught here!

The police sirens keened again... ominously close!

# CHAPTER 2
# TORTURE CLUE

THE WAIL of those sirens crept into the warmly lighted dining room of the Frisco Club, too. In a corner behind potted palms a woman listened intently during an infrequent intermission of music. She sat more erectly in her chair and peered across the floor toward the exit through which Richard Wentworth had disappeared.

The woman, Nita van Sloan, rose deliberately. She picked up her evening bag and through its fabric felt the outline of a small automatic. If there was fear in her heart, the serene beauty of her face hid it completely. She walked across the dining room along the path Wentworth had taken... too long ago.

Men's heads swung to follow her, approving. Women's eyes were envious. Nita van Sloan carried herself with the pride of a princess, and the beauty of her face, framed in chestnut curls, came from a great heart as much as from perfection of features. She was a fit mate for the Spider... the one woman to whom he had given his confidence and his love.

She knew now, as surely as if spoken words had passed between them, that Richard Wentworth was in danger! When that peril struck, she would be at his side—as was her right and her desire.

Once out of sight of the diners, Nita moved more rapidly. A man, hand thrust deep in his pocket, stepped from a dark corner of the hallway.

"Wait a minute, sister," he said flatly.

Nita turned her violet eyes upon him without concern. The man's face broke suddenly into a smile.

"Oh, excuse me, Miss van Sloan!" the man said. "I didn't know it was you. Briscoe gave us strict orders."

Nita nodded without words and went on to the door of Briscoe's office. She drew her long kid gloves over her hand before she touched the knob. It did not turn.

Alarm shot through Nita. Her taut nerves brought her the knowledge that the police sirens were in the street before the club now, would soon whine to a halt. She half-turned toward the corner, around which the guard stood… and she felt the knob turn!

Nita stepped swiftly back across the width of the hall, and her hand slid into her bag, closed firmly about the automatic. The door opened—and Richard Wentworth stepped quietly across the threshold!

He surveyed Nita with a steely look, then a smile moved his lips. "I might have known you would come," he said gently. "Let's get back to our table, quickly!"

Nita fell into step beside him. "Guard around the corner," she said, her voice no more than a sigh in his ear. "Briscoe's man… saw me come."

Wentworth spun on his heel. His hand turned Nita with him.

"We'll go through the women's room," he formed soundless words. "It has exits on both corridors!"

Nita went first through the doorway. An instant later there were thin, piping cries… and Nita opened the door for Wentworth.

"It was curious," Nita smiled up at him. "As soon as I came in here, I saw the most fortuitous mouse! There were only two women and the attendant… and none of them stayed to investigate!"

They went through the restroom quickly. Wentworth's lips stirred in faint acknowledgment of Nita's cleverness, but his eyes were cold. Rapidly he told Nita what had happened in Briscoe's office.

Nita sucked in a quick breath at the news of the stolen gun. "It killed Briscoe… and it has your fingerprints!" she whispered. **WENTWORTH BOWED** her into her chair at their hidden corner table. "That's unimportant at present," he said. "What is important, is this: *Judge Torture must be wiped out!*"

Nita's worried eyes softened as she looked into the strong and resolute face of the man she loved. It was so like him, thrusting aside personal danger to take the trail of the enemies of mankind! She saw Wentworth's face stiffen as he stared out across the dining room. Carelessly, he changed his seat to the one beside her.

"Inspector Littlejohn is standing in the main doorway," he said softly. "One man on the police force who does not particularly like me!"

Nita's hand closed tightly over Wentworth's. As usual, Dick

16

was guilty of understatement. Littlejohn had practically sworn a vendetta against him, because Wentworth had solved certain cases to Littlejohn's detriment. He was one of few police who persisted in connecting Wentworth with the Spider, despite the multiple proofs that apparently had been offered to the contrary.

"Dick," Nita whispered, "you'll have to leave! I'll stay here and try to find out about that gun!"

Wentworth nodded gravely. "That may be necessary. If it is, you will say that you are waiting here for me. I do not like the looks of those three men who just trailed Briscoe's fiancée to her table."

Nita's glance followed Wentworth's nod. She saw an exquisitely gowned girl occupy a remote table, alone. "Roberta Swan," she said. "I knew she sang here, but I didn't know she and Briscoe were engaged."

The girl was brunette, with hair of midnight blackness and her dress was flame red. She was vivid enough to dominate even that brilliance... but just now her face was dead white as she looked at the three men who were sitting down at her table. There was a menacing aura about the trio. Roberta Swan sat rigidly, hands upon the table.

"I think," Wentworth said quietly, "that we should offer our congratulations to Miss Swan."

Nita's hand clutched at Wentworth's arm. "But Littlejohn!"

17

Wentworth moved a hand impatiently. "I'm watching him. He's moving down the corridor toward Briscoe's office."

"Miss Swan is safe, Dick," Nita insisted. "Those three men must be some of Briscoe's guards!"

Wentworth shook his head. "There's something wrong, Nita. I identified the dead bailiff of Judge Torture," he said. "He is Pete Louis. And one of those three men over there is Pete Louis' inseparable companion. Slash Franker—he is very handy… with a knife."

Wentworth and Nita had risen when the three men stood up beside Roberta Swan's table. Between them, Wentworth saw the girl suddenly clasp her hands to her breast. She set her teeth violently on her lower lip, and a drop of blood squeezed out of the flesh, trickled down her chin. She made no sound.

THE THREE men turned away and swaggered across the dining room. Roberta Swan sat as they had left her. She took one hand away from her breast, and dabbed at her lip. Her eyes were staring wide, glassy with terror or pain. She swayed to her feet. One hand still pressed against her breast, she moved stiffly across the dining room in the wake of the three men!

Wentworth's voice was brittle. "Stay here, Nita!" he directed, and she knew that she must obey.

Nita van Sloan turned back to her table in the corner. Her eyes were dark with fright as she watched Wentworth stride after the automaton-like girl. Yet when Inspector Littlejohn came, as he would, Nita must be surprised and gay….

"Why, good evening, Inspector! Won't you sit down? Mr. Wentworth will be here almost any minute now…."

18

Nita dropped her forehead against a braced palm. A sob struggled in her throat. "Oh, Dick, be careful!" she whispered. "Be careful! There is… *danger!*"

Roberta Swan had almost reached the main doorway of the dining room when Wentworth overtook her. "Good evening, Roberta!" he said quietly. "I understand we are to offer you congratulations!"

Roberta Swan's head swung about. The cut on her lower lip showed a trace of blood, and her hand still pressed hard into her breast. Her eyes held no recognition at all. They held only terror. She did not speak… and Wentworth's nostrils arched in sudden horror.

He could not be mistaken. There was an odor here… an odor of burned flesh! *Human flesh!*

Wentworth's eyes fixed on Roberta's left hand, pressed where her low gown swung across the curve of a lovely breast. He knew, with a terrible surety, what had happened. One of those three men also carried the tipstaff of Judge Torture. He had used it on this girl, to inflict a burn upon her breast! And she was still following the pull of that fearful tipstaff!

Wentworth said, gently, "You do not have to follow those men, Roberta! I will protect you!"

Roberta did not answer. They had reached the cloakroom now, and the three men stood at the head of the steps that led down to the street. The check girl came out with Roberta's evening wrap. Roberta caught it hurriedly high about her throat… but not before Wentworth had seen the confirmation of his suspicions! There, on the white flesh of the girl's breast, was a deep and angry burn!

Wentworth swung toward the three men… but they were already moving down the steps! Wentworth's left arm clamped down on the gun beneath his left armpit… Briscoe's gun, which he had snatched up from the office floor. His lips drew into a determined line, and there was deep concern in his kind eyes.

He would save Roberta, but first he must subject her to even graver danger! For those three men, and Roberta, would lead him to Judge Torture!

Wentworth caught up his light topcoat and silk hat from the counter of the cloakroom, rapidly donned them. He took his slim, black gold-headed cane into his fist and he thought comfortably of the slender, honed rapier the cane concealed!

"I haven't been here, tonight," he said softly to the checkroom girl, and laid a ten dollar bill on the counter.

The girl nodded alertly. They were loyal to Joseph Briscoe here, and they knew Wentworth was his friend. She would obey.

A half dozen paces behind Roberta Swan, Wentworth moved toward the steps. Roberta was below, just inside the door.

At this moment, gunfire crashed out in the street!

ROBERTA SWAN did not even check her deliberate slow pacing toward the door. She thrust open the glass panel and a bullet smashed through it. A starred fracture splintered the pane within inches of her hand. Roberta did not flinch. Her hand did not move aside. She went out onto the sidewalk.

Wentworth cried out to her and went down the steps in a long bound. Through the swinging glass door, he saw the entire scene in the street. There were three uniformed police crouched down on the pavement. One had thrown himself behind a parked car. They were firing toward a big refrigerated butcher's truck across the street, and from its rear aperture the stab of gun-flame answered them!

Even as Wentworth bounded to the walk, Roberta staggered and reeled aside. She flung an arm toward a stanchion supporting the awning over the walk. She caught it and pivoted around the upright, backward, as gracefully as a dancer on her partner's hand. But her knees were buckling. Her head was thrown back so that the strained cords of her throat stood out in the shadowed light.

She was suddenly flat upon the pavement. Her skirts settled about her with a faint rustling. The bullet wound in her breast had stabbed a red period into the burn from Judge Torture's tipstaff!

Furiously, Wentworth whirled toward that blasting killer's gun across the street. His hand whipped toward his underarm holster, but he didn't draw. At that instant a police bullet pierced the killer's brain. The gunman pitched out from behind the truck, and two more police bullets found him in the same moment. The police pelted across the street, shouting, guns glinting in their hands!

Wentworth heard, seemingly from behind the truck, a clatter of steel. It echoed hollowly above the noise of running policemen. No more gunshots sounded.

Wentworth started away from the doorway. There was nothing more he could do here… and two of the killers of Judge Torture had escaped! There was a trail the Spider must follow!

But footsteps were pounding within the club, and men were shouting there. Before he could get out of sight, they would be after him. A slight smile stirred Wentworth's lips. He sprang to the curb, whipped open the door of an abandoned taxi. He knuckled his silk hat to the back of his head, tucked his cane beneath his arm… and suddenly the dapperness was gone from his appearance. His shoulders were no longer alert, and his head wobbled.

"No sense to it," he said thickly toward the driver's seat. "I demand to know the amount of my fare. Keep me standing here where… where bullets and things are." He hammered on the edge of the door with a fumbling fist! "I'll report you, s'help me, I'll report you! Insubordinate, that's what… what you are!" WENTWORTH TURNED away from the cab, and wavered a little in his stride. A policeman bounded toward him, with a gun in his fist. Wentworth ignored the gun. He waved toward the cab.

"Confounded driver won't tell me what I owe him," he complained. "As an officer, I appeal to you! Call you to witness, I won't pay him!"

The policeman grinned slightly. "All right, Mac," he said. "We'll take care of it. Better get along now."

"Going into Frisco Club," Wentworth said.

"Oh, no you aren't!" The policeman caught him by the arm and spun him away from the door. "Come along now, get going! You might get hurt!"

Wentworth reeled about in an erratic circle, swung back toward the cop. "Demand to go into the club," he said vociferously. "Lady waiting for me. Gentleman never neglect a lady!"

"Shove off!" the cop said irritably. "Got other things to attend to now. Damn it, shove off, or I'll run you in!"

Wentworth stumbled off up the street, heard the police grumble to another cop about a "damned drunk!"

Wentworth's eyes were unamused as he kept up the pretense of drunkenness. One way of getting out of a tight jam was to force the police to put you out! But he had accomplished his purpose. He was on the trail of Judge Torture!

He glanced across the street toward the rear of the parked butcher truck. That sound of hollow clanging steel puzzled him. He doubted if the two killers had had time enough to escape from the street before he himself had emerged from the club. His conjecture regarding the truck was soon abandoned, however, because policemen stepped to the truck, inspected its interior, and found nothing.

Wentworth's eyes combed the opposite side of the street, and slowly a smile pulled at his lips. There was a butcher shop on the corner, and it had steel trapdoors that opened in the sidewalk. They would make, in rapid closing, such a sound as he had heard. And they would have been concealed from the police by the butcher's truck. Butcher shop, and butcher truck—that was no accident!

Wentworth puckered his lips and whistled softly into the night a doleful, wailing tune. He reached the corner and wavered there uncertainly, still enacting his drunken role.

23

From the darkness around the corner, there came the soft closing of an auto door. In the shadows was the bulk of a long, powerful limousine, and it was from this car that a man came bounding forward in answer to that whistle. The man's head was bound in a white turban, and his eyes glittered eagerly above the thicket of a Sikh's beard. He was Wentworth's chauffeur—and his comrade at arms!

"*Han, sahib!*" cried Ram Singh, his deep voice muted to a rumble. "I heard my master's signal! Do we fight?"

Wentworth answered him in the explosive Punjabi which was Ram Singh's native language. "Nay, thou bloodthirsty one, not now," he said. "But two men who richly deserve death have taken refuge in the basement of that butcher shop on the corner. See thou that they do not leave their lair!"

RAM SINGH'S teeth flashed white behind the black beard, and his hand caressed the hilt of a great Khyber knife thrust under his sash. "Nay, master," he grumbled. "Why wait? Let thy servant go into this rat nest and destroy these mice who, in this effete land, call themselves killers!"

Wentworth's lips parted in a slow appreciative smile. "Wait, thou lion warrior, and watch!" he said. "I need those men alive. Take this gun and holster, for presently I shall be searched... And take this cigarette, Ram Singh!"

"A cigarette, *sahib!*"

Wentworth nodded. "It is one of my special cigarettes, Ram Singh, so do not try to smoke it! Presently, Kirkpatrick *sahib* will come to the club. Five minutes after his entrance, do you light this cigarette and drop it into that basement! It will smoke out your… rats!"

*"Han, sahib!"* Ram Singh swept his hands to his forehead in an elaborate salaam. There was nothing servile about this great-hearted Sikh… but he gave allegiance to a greater warrior than he! To the Master of Men!

Wentworth turned away from the corner, behind which Ram Singh still lurked. He glared back toward the awning marquee of the Frisco Club. Then he began his meandering march back toward the entrance!

"Look here!" he demanded of the policeman on guard. "I'm going into the club and be damned to you! Your chief knows me… Richard Wentworth!… I tell you, my good fellow, a gentleman doesn't keep a lady waiting!"

He took his wavering, deliberate way toward the door… and the police stepped aside.

## CHAPTER 3
## TORTURE PAY-OFF

ONCE WENTWORTH was past the outer guard, the police did not interfere with him. A patrolman at the head of the steps saluted him. In the dining hall, people sat glumly at their tables; the bar was noisy.

Wentworth's eyes went at once to Nita's table and relief flooded through him. She was smiling gaily up into the face of Inspector Littlejohn!

Wentworth made his way directly to the table. "I'm sorry to

be late, in' dear," he said, with deliberately blurred articulation. "Stupid police at the door wouldn't let me in."

Littlejohn cut in, ironically. "The stupid police were following my stupid orders, Mr. Wentworth!"

Wentworth's head swung about. "Ah, Littlejohn… Yes, I should have known you were here!" He made a small bow, and swayed off balance. Nita caught his arm, eased him into a chair.

# JUDGEMENT OF THE DAMNED

Masked policemen, machine guns in hand, rushed toward the cellar opening...

27

Littlejohn had a long dour face and small eyes that were like bright blue fires. "Never saw you drunk before, Mr. Wentworth," he said.

"Stupid police," Wentworth said again. "I'm not drunk. Not drunk at all! Nita, tell the inspector you've never seen me drunk."

Nita laughed gently, "I'm surprised at you, Inspector Littlejohn," she said.

A slight flush crept into Littlejohn's long face. His voice hardened. "Mr. Wentworth, have you a gun?"

"Dozens of them, my dear Littlejohn," Wentworth laughed. "And all authentically licensed."

Littlejohn said, shortly, "I'll trouble you for the one you're carrying now... and the license!"

Wentworth nodded carelessly, fumbled into his inside pocket. He flipped out a wallet. "License in there, Littlejohn," he said, and reached under his left arm. A blank look came across his face. Then he began to laugh uproariously. "F' heaven's sake!" he chortled. "Imagine carrying a license and no gun! I remember now. Someone stole the gun. I intended to report it tonight."

Littlejohn's eyes blazed with concentration. "Stole your gun, where?" he snapped.

Wentworth's eyes were owlish. "My dear Inspector," he said. "If I knew where the gun was stolen, I could catch the thief myself... Stupid question." He turned to Nita. "It's the gun I usually keep in the limousine. Handy little affair... Thirty-eight with a test barrel."

Littlejohn leaned across the table. "In your forgetful mood,

Mr. Wentworth," he said, slowly, "you didn't put on your holster, and forget to put in the gun, did you?"

Wentworth blinked at him. "Now, I wonder…" He pulled the left lapel of his coat wide and peered down where the holster would hang. "No, inspector… It seems not."

Littlejohn straightened, managing to withhold an angry oath.

"We'll find your gun, Mr. Wentworth!" he snapped. "And when we do, you'll have some questions to answer!… Joseph Briscoe was murdered tonight… with a thirty-eight caliber bullet!"

Wentworth went through histrionics of surprise and Little-john stormed away, just as Commissioner Stanley Kirkpatrick showed himself in the doorway of the dining hall.

Nita laid a hand on Wentworth's arm. "You won't be able to fool Stanley Kirkpatrick like that, Dick," she said. She smoth-ered a giggle. "Littlejohn was so angry! Dick, you should be ashamed of yourself!"

Wentworth rose to his feet. "Come with me to talk to Kirk, dear," he said. "This has got to be fast from now on. I tracked down those crooks. Ram Singh is on guard."

HE STRODE with sharp decision across the dining room, and found Kirkpatrick's impassive gaze upon him before he was half way across. Littlejohn swung about, anger still in his cheeks.

"Wentworth!" he snapped. "You were pretending to be drunk!"

Wentworth lifted his brows at Littlejohn. "Really, Littlejohn! I assured you I was not drunk… had never been drunk in my life… and Miss van Sloan confirmed me! If your observations were faulty, you cannot blame me! Kirk…."

There was a hint of a smile on Kirkpatrick's long straight mouth. He knuckled his mustache to conceal it.

"What are you up to, Dick?" he asked quietly.

Wentworth said, crisply, "I walked into the shooting outside the door of the club, Kirk. Didn't participate because I didn't have my gun, as I was explaining to Inspector Littlejohn. I had a theory I wanted to check on immediately; I feigned drunkenness so that the police at the door would not detain me. I verified that theory... and I can locate for you the thugs who are responsible for Briscoe's death, I believe, and who certainly killed the girl at the door."

Kirkpatrick's voice was stern. "Was the subterfuge necessary with Inspector Littlejohn?"

Wentworth smiled, glanced toward Littlejohn. "I'm afraid the inspector doesn't think very well of me, Kirk," he said. "My apologies, Inspector... I didn't want to go into this twice. Kirk, the gunman who fought the police took refuge behind a butcher truck conveniently parked across the street. Two others disappeared on an empty street... and there is a butcher shop on the corner, whose basement entrance is concealed behind the truck!"

Kirkpatrick frowned in concentration. "A curious coincidence, at least!"

"Moreover," Wentworth sped on, "I heard a hollow reverberation of steel... as of sidewalk trapdoors slammed down in a hurry!"

Kirkpatrick snapped an order at Littlejohn, and the inspector dashed off to assemble men. "But, confound it, Dick," Kirkpatrick said, "the men may have escaped while you delayed!"

Wentworth smiled slightly, "Do you think Littlejohn would have acted with your admirable promptitude, Kirk? The inspector, Kirk, does me the honor to suspect me of being the Spider! He has told me so!"

Kirkpatrick sniffed, "Still, Dick, the men could have escaped from that basement!"

Wentworth's smile broadened, "With Ram Singh on guard, Kirk?"

Kirkpatrick laughed sharply. "Dick, you're incurable! And all this, while my men thought you were a stupid drunk! They told me about you!" He sobered. "It isn't to be wondered, Dick, that men as keen as Little John… and myself… occasionally suspect you of being the Spider!"

Wentworth shrugged, with irritation. "I grow weary of that kind of talk," he said tartly. "There have been proofs!"

Kirkpatrick nodded. "Proofs that you were not the Spider, and never a shred of conclusive evidence that you were. I hope, Dick, for both our sakes… that the evidence of your guilt never falls into my hands!" He swung about. "Coming on this raid, Dick?"

Wentworth's voice was still sharp, "I think I'll just keep myself clear of suspicion for once," he said. "Nita, shall we keep our engagement… elsewhere than at the Frisco?"

Nita's hand rested on his arm. "Of course, Dick," she said.

Kirkpatrick's eyes rested on Wentworth through a long moment. "Dick, see that you do stay… clear of suspicion! Patrolman Carter!" he called to the cop on guard at the steps. "Permit Mr. Wentworth and Miss van Sloan to leave!"

As they went down the steps, Wentworth glanced covertly at his watch. He figured that Ram Singh must have tossed the cigarette into the cellar two minutes earlier… He had timed it well. Passing out the front door, Wentworth was once more uncertain in his pace. He peered owlishly at the police on guard there… turned up the street with Nita laughing on his arm.

"It wouldn't do," he whispered, "to let these men know they were tricked. I might not be able to trick them so easily next time!"

"But how about Littlejohn, Dick!" Nita protested.

Wentworth smiled slightly, "It's easy to fool clever men," he said. "You merely tell them the truth… and their own cleverness tricks them. They know that, under the same circumstances, they would not tell the truth!"

WENTWORTH WHISTLED softly the signal to Ram Singh… police were already forming a swift cordon around the butcher shop… and the Sikh strode out of the shadows. His salaam to Nita was respectful. *Wah*, she was a woman even a warrior of the Sikhs might honor! Had not even he, Ram Singh, taken her orders and found them such as a brave man might accept?

"No one left the shop, Ram Singh?" Wentworth asked.

"The mice kept to their hole, *sahib!*" There was regret in Ram Singh's voice.

32

Wentworth nodded his praise and went directly to his limousine. Once they were inside, he spoke his quiet orders to Ram Singh… "Six blocks away, Ram Singh, and return!" With his left hand, he pulled out an ashtray, twisted it to the right and then the left. A second glass panel slid up inside of each window—and they were suddenly opaque!*

Nita said, "Oh, Dick! But… the Spider walk tonight? Kirkpatrick is watching you closely!"

Wentworth's lips twisted in a slight smile. He sat on a kick seat, and at his touch of another hidden switch, the left half of the rear cushion slid forward, revolved, and revealed a closely packed wardrobe… a lighted makeup tray.

"Kirkpatrick is always watching, dear," he said quietly. "I am not satisfied about that basement hideout… nor that the police will ferret all its secrets. And Judge Torture must be tracked down at once! The man is too powerful! God alone knows what havoc he will wreak… if the Spider does not walk!"

As he spoke, he was swiftly at work before the mirror of his makeup tray. Under his deft hands, the lines of his kindly, intelligent face became strangely altered… and there peered back from him, in the glass, the ominous, beaked and ruthless coun-

---

* AUTHOR'S NOTE: This was a new installation and Wentworth found it much more efficient than the older, automatically operated shades. Each pane of glass was of Polaroid, which stratified the light rays. Either window, used alone, permitted clear vision. But when both were used, with their strata, of filtered light at right-angles, not a gleam of interior of exterior illumination could pass through them.

33

tenance of... the Spider! He whipped a heel-length cape from the wardrobe, dragged a broad-brimmed hat down over his eyes. A wig made his hair lank and long; his brows were bushy ridges.

At his touch, the second Polaroid panel sank back into its socket, and he saw that the car was just returning to a street a block from where they had started. He had timed it perfectly.

"Nita," he said quietly, "I know it is useless to attempt to send you to safety. Pass through one of these streets at intervals of two minutes. The signal will be a double flicker of my flashlight."

Nita's hand clung to his. Wordlessly, she offered her lips to the kiss of the Spider.

In the darkness of the street, the long black limousine hesitated for an instant. There was no sound of opened or closed door, and only the shadows seemed to shift and settle back upon themselves. But when the limousine passed the next corner, Nita was alone in the rear of the car!

COMMISSIONER KIRKPATRICK reached the street in time to see the first disappearance of Wentworth's car. There was tightness about his lips, and worry in his eyes. Too many times Wentworth had disappeared from the scene of a crime—and the Spider soon thereafter made his appearance! Kirkpatrick shook his head sharply, as if to rid himself of unpleasant thoughts, and strode toward the corner butcher shop.

His keen eyes skipped over the lines of his men, lifted to the roof to spot the silhouette of ready guards there. Yes, the place was surrounded. If Wentworth were right, and his deduction seemed sound, the killers would still be in the basement.

Inspector Littlejohn stepped to his side.

"All set, Commissioner," he reported.

Kirkpatrick nodded and gestured toward the twin steel trap-doors in the sidewalk.

"Open them," he ordered his men. "Give the men a chance to surrender. If they refuse, use tear gas."

Once more he glanced about him, swore softly under his breath. If Wentworth tried that Spider trick again tonight, there would be an end of him! Kirkpatrick pulled back his shoulders against a vast weight that seemed to settle upon them. If Dick would only give up this madness of his! Side by side, within the law....

Kirkpatrick smiled grimly. Wentworth had an adequate respect for the law, but it was his custom to point out that the law was a means, not an end in itself. Justice was the ideal! Both of them, warm friends and implacable enemies, served that ideal, each in his own fashion!

Littlejohn's voice was crisp as he ordered the trapdoors opened. Two men crouched over the doors, sprang back as they wrenched them wide... and black smoke belched upward from the opening!

"Fire!" Littlejohn rasped. "Turn in an alarm!"

"Hold it!" Kirkpatrick stepped quietly forward. He peered at the curling vapors. A vagrant wind scooped up black smoke, whirled it toward him. Kirkpatrick's nostrils curled. He swore and stepped back.

"That's not fire, Inspector," he said sharply. "It's a smoke bomb with a particularly vile stench! The Spider once used such a bomb!"

Littlejohn rasped out an oath. "Emergency wagon!" he snapped. "Put in a call! Tell them to bring extra smoke helmets!" KIRKPATRICK LET the order go through, and while he waited, he paced slowly up and down the pavement. At every turn the police ran into traces of the Spider. His seal was on the forehead of that curiously dressed dead man in the office of the slain Briscoe. But the police could testify that Wentworth arrived, from outside, at the door of the club… Child's play, of course, for the Spider. But Briscoe had been Wentworth's protégé, and he had gone straight since his release from prison.

The hoarse siren of the emergency wagon heralded its arrival and the big green truck slammed into the street. Orders rang crisply. Great searchlights threw their brilliant rays into the swirling smoke. Helmeted men, machine guns in their hands, marched toward the opening. No one answered the shouted order to come out. The police went into the cellar doorway.

It was perhaps a minute later that one of the helmeted men came staggering back into sight. He groped at the chute down which packages were slid to the basement. He gripped it desperately, fought his way upward.

"Help that man!" Kirkpatrick ordered.

The man sprawled on his stomach on the pavement, struggled to his feet. Desperately, he clawed at the helmet on his head. It came free in his hand and he staggered to the curb, leaned against the truck and was violently sick.

"What's the matter, Carroll?" Kirkpatrick cried urgently. "Is that gas poisonous? Does your helmet leak?"

The man shook his head, managed to turn presently to the

36

Commissioner. His face was greenish, and his eyes were strained wide.

"It's not that, Commissioner," he said weakly. "It's—it's what we found down there! God, I—" He leaned against the truck again.

Kirkpatrick knuckled the spiked ends of his mustache and worry drew a knife-crease between his brows. He waited patiently. He knew Carroll, as he made it his business to know most of the men of his entire force. Carroll was no weakling, but it was obvious that there was horror beyond the capacity of his resistance in that black, smoking hole.

Kirkpatrick watched that black hole, and schooled himself with his iron-hard control. Presently Carroll was at his side. "I'm sorry, Commissioner," he said hoarsely. "Down in that basement, two men—they've been tortured to death. It's pretty gruesome, sir."

Kirkpatrick said harshly, "Give me a helmet, Carroll!"

The brilliant light washed over Kirkpatrick's upright figure as he strode toward the trapdoor. His shoulders were stiff. He ignored the hand that a policeman held out to help him, sprang nimbly down into the darkness. He stepped from the entrance well into the main cellar. Lights burned smokily in the ceiling now. Powerful flashlights focused on the wall across the room, and....

Kirkpatrick's oath echoed deafeningly in his ears beneath the helmet. He took a long stride forward, checked. He felt a fist knot about his heart and squeeze coldly, and all his body was

37

rigid with contracted horror. Carroll had said it was horrible. But this... this was the work of a monster from hell!

TWO MEN had been tortured to death, and at least one of them had died in wasting agony. One leg had been severed at the knee, and the other was mangled. Great spikes penetrated his body. He had been crucified, but not upon a cross. Instead, his body was impaled against a frame that formed a capital letter G.

His broken neck dangled to form the tip of the G, his back was horribly arched into the curve and his knee bent backward to form the upright of the letter. There was evidence that this had been done while the man was still alive.

But the other man—his body had been segmented to form a letter N. His legs, cut off at the thighs, were the uprights. His torso, horribly pierced, was the oblique bar.

Angrily, Kirkpatrick ripped off the helmet. The swirling fumes choked him, made his eyes sting, but it was more endurable than the closeness beneath the helmet. He could not breathe right. His heart hammered, fiercely.

"In God's name!" he whispered.

A helmeted policeman stepped to his side. His voice came out tinnily through the speech diaphragm. "Trapdoors seem to be the only exit except through the store, Commissioner," he reported. "All doors up there are locked tight."

Kirkpatrick said, harshly, "Those men didn't do that to themselves! This place has been under constant surveillance ever since two men entered here. Look for a hidden doorway... a tunnel!"

He staggered back to the trapdoor and his face, peering up toward Littlejohn on the pavement, was drawn with stern lines.

"Get the technical men over from the Frisco Club, Littlejohn," he ordered. "Extend the cordon to cover a full block on each side of this place. Looks like a tunnel connection. One of the dead men is Slash Franker... a partner of the man whom the Spider killed at the club."

Little John's hot eyes flashed. "You mean the Spider has turned to torture now!"

Kirkpatrick snapped, "Good God, no! The Spider never did a thing like this! Hurry!"

He turned back into the basement. It was when he was half-way across the basement that he heard the laughter. It swelled from the smoky darkness, sibilant, flat and mocking!

A policeman swore through his diaphragm. "The Spider he cried. "It's the Spider!"

Snouted machine guns combed the darkness, but found no target. The laughter broke off and the Spider's voice whispered into the darkness!

"A word for you, Kirkpatrick," it whispered. "The man who did this is known as Judge Torture. If you are curious about the meaning of those two human initials, ponder this. The men failed in their task, which was to kidnap Joseph Briscoe! It suggests that Judge Torture has a macabre sense of humor, Kirkpatrick... N.G. means *No Good!*"

Kirkpatrick's voice rasped out. "Search this basement! There is a secret exit! The Spider is in it!"

"Don't move!" The Spider's voice rapped out. "My guns are on you... Kirkpatrick, just one word more, and I'll take my leave! I know very little more about this than you. I found this tunnel by dropping a stench bomb into the basement and smelling out the exit in a nearby tenement!… Don't give the obvious order, Kirkpatrick!… One word more. The G of the initials had no part in the fracas at the Frisco Club. I think you will find the leg in Briscoe's office is his! I can identify him for you. He is the brother of Morris Bacon, the philanthropist!

"And Kirkpatrick, warn your men—if any one points a tiny wand tipped with metal at them, they are to shoot—to kill!"

Once more the sibilant mocking laughter of the Spider rang through the smoky basement, and then there was silence!

Instantly, Kirkpatrick snapped out orders. "The right wall!" he cried. "Corner to the rear! That's where the Spider was! There's a secret opening there! Find it!… Little John—throw men into the buildings north of here! The Spider is racing through an underground tunnel to one of those buildings!"

**RUNNING SWIFTLY** through the tunnel, Wentworth heard the cries of Commissioner Kirkpatrick fade out behind him. The swift impact of pickaxes ringing on the entrance to the passage echoed with him as he sped on. It would take close timing but he would reach the end of the tunnel before Little-john could plug it. If Nita was in the street beyond, with the car, he would be safe. If not….

Wentworth thrust the worry from his mind. There was horror in his soul over the fearful scene in that basement torture room. And Judge Torture had been clever. He had left no clues… not even with the men who had exposed themselves in the Frisco Club. One remained unaccounted for, but Wentworth had no doubt that he, too, had paid the penalty of failure!

Wentworth's flashlight penetrated the darkness ahead and he skated to a halt beside the section of brick wall that formed the door. Swiftly, his hand flew to the operating lever. The wall pivoted easily, and behind him, a dim shout rang out! The police had broken through the end of the tunnel!

Wentworth sped through the opening, swung the door shut. He had deliberately led the police to this tunnel so that a secret of Judge Torture might be revealed, but they were coming faster than he had anticipated. The doors of the trap were closing about the Spider! Two long bounds took him toward the steps that led to the street level. Now he ran in darkness, avoiding obstacles with his unerring memory for a scene once viewed… and sound beat softly on his ears from the steps!

Wentworth halted. His automatic flipped into his hand… but he did not fire! That man on the steps might be a policeman, and the Spider did not war on the police even to save his own life!

The Spider hesitated… and from the steps, a gun spat crimson flame into the darkness!

It would have been simple for Wentworth, with his unerring accuracy, to have put a bullet through the man who fired. He did not. Instead, he plucked out a small capsule from the leather girdle he wore. He flicked the capsule toward the steps, and it burst there with a tiny burst of flame and a muffled detonation.

Wentworth's lips curved thinly… and in the darkness, a man swore on a thin note. He coughed and gasped. Feet clattered on the steps. A door opened and banged. Tear gas had routed the enemy!

Dick Wentworth muffled his face in the robe he wore,

leaped toward the steps, and once more he checked. Heavy feet pounded overhead. There were hoarse shouts! Littlejohn had arrived with the police!

Behind Dick there was the dull sound of iron striking against the secret brick door which he had jammed shut!

The only two exits to the basement were closed!

## CHAPTER 4
## SPIDER AT BAY

INSPECTOR LITTLEJOHN stood in the first floor hall of the tenement, his legs braced wide apart. His gun was in his fist as his blazing blue eyes peered into the darkness. His men scattered through the building.

Littlejohn sniffed the air. There was the usual stale dankness of tenement halls, but there was another, more acrid scent. It rasped in his throat, stung his eyes.

"This is the building!" Littlejohn swore harshly. "The Spider's exit has to be through this basement!"

His voice lifted in sharp orders, dispatching men to all exits. His gun muzzle was centered on the basement door. The tear gas puzzled him. It was true that he thought he had heard a muffled gunshot just before he burst into the hallway. The devil! Was he already too late?

Men were racing through the tunnel from the butcher shop. If he did not move fast, and the Spider was still in the trap, they would get the Spider first!

That was something Inspector Littlejohn did not intend to let happen.

"To hell with the tear gas," he muttered.

He seized the basement door and wrenched it open. A swirl of grayish vapor curled around his legs. It was thin and it dissipated quickly in the draft through the hall. Littlejohn shouted and leaped down the basement steps, gun-first!

Littlejohn's voice rang out sharply in the basement. "Hold everything in the tunnel!" he cried. "I'm down here! And I'll get the Spider!"

He coughed rackingly and his flashlight beam swept about the basement, searching. His gun was nervous in his fist. He cursed as he stomped about, poking into the coal bin, clattering among stacked trunks.

At the head of the steps a policeman waited grimly. He held a sub-machine gun in his hands. The thinning tear gas worked on his eyes and nostrils, making them sting. He swore warily, backed a few feet away from the opening. He could hear Littlejohn curse and cough and curse again. He could hear the chink of steel against the bricks where the tunnel crew was still working on the door.

The cop was a little afraid. The Spider was a mysterious man in a black robe, who killed whenever his guns spoke. He had never seen the Spider; he didn't particularly want to. They said around the station house that the Spider never killed cops, but you couldn't tell about a thing like that. Put a guy in a tight spot, put a gun in his fist, and he'd kill anybody to get out.

That was natural.

43

The cop's hands whitened with their grip on the machine gun as he caught the stamp of feet on the steps, then he heard cursing and coughing again.

"Look out, up there!" came the hoarse order. "And don't blaze away at me!"

THE COP crouched and the muzzle of the machine gun wavered a little with his tension. You had to watch this Spider. He was tricky!

"You come up slow," he snapped, "so I can see if you're Inspector Littlejohn!"

The swearing came up the steps. At the head, where the tear gas was thickest, the footsteps stopped. The cop sidled across the hall, machine gun ready. Then he grunted and relief relaxed his tension.

"Excuse me, Inspector," he said, "but I had to make sure."

"All right, all right!" the figure stumbled into the hallway, racked with coughing. "Got to get some clean air. Keep your eye on this door!"

He stumbled past the cop toward the back door, and the cop glanced at him, then back at the basement steps. Slowly, tension gripped him again. He cleared his throat a little. Inspector Littlejohn must have a mighty tender throat. Tear gas didn't get the cop like it did the inspector. The cop felt a little proud....

In the back yard, the man in Inspector Littlejohn's clothing recovered rapidly. He strode angrily past the guard placed there,

44

acknowledged the man's salute brusquely and went on into the next street. He turned a corner, and presently a black limousine slid along the street. A light flicked twice in his fist, and the limousine slid to a halt!

He sprang into the back seat. A woman cried out softly, in alarm… and then she laughed. A man's laughter joined with hers and the limousine picked up speed. As it swept away from the police cordon, a rattle-trap coupé skittered out of a dark side street and rumbled along in its wake….

BACK IN the hallway of the tenement, the cop jerked at the sound of footsteps in the hallway, then stiffened to salute as Commissioner Kirkpatrick came striding through.

"Where's Littlejohn?" Kirkpatrick demanded sharply.

"Went out back, sir," the cop reported crisply. "Got a dose of tear gas and had to have some air."

"Tear gas!" Kirkpatrick snapped, incredulously.

He sniffed the air, caught the acrid whiff of the vapor. "Doesn't seem to be very strong," he said, gruffly. "You been bothered?"

The cop said, slowly, "No, sir. Maybe the inspector has a tender throat. He was coughing an awful lot!"

Kirkpatrick rapped out an oath. "Did Littlejohn go down in that basement alone?"

"Yes, sir," the cop stammered.

Kirkpatrick spun on the men behind him. "Quickly!" he snapped. "Out back! It's probably too late, but search every-where! The Spider made a get-away in Littlejohn's clothes! I say there—Sergeant Reams!"

## THE SPIDER

"Here, sir!" a grave-faced sergeant in uniform stepped to his side.

"Get your gun out, Sergeant Reams, and follow me," Kirkpatrick ordered.

He took the sergeant's big-barreled flashlight, sent its wide beam into the basement obscurity and went down rapidly. He swung the beam once across the basement, checked with an oath and stood staring.

Propped against the opposite wall was Inspector Littlejohn! The Spider's hat was on his head and it was twisted into a grotesque imitation of Napoleon's conventional military hat. Littlejohn's hand was tucked into the front of his shirt and the Spider's cape was about his shoulders. Littlejohn's uniform was gone!

There was a placard in his lap. It read:

*"Confucius say: Wise men walk alone only when calling on lady friend."*

It was signed with the seal of the Spider!

A snort of laughter broke Kirkpatrick's gravity, but he strangled it swiftly. There was a broad grin on Sergeant Reams' usually grave face.

Kirkpatrick swung toward him. "Not a word about this, Sergeant! Although it would serve Littlejohn right—dashing down here alone! This craze to catch the Spider becomes an obsession with some men…" His voice turned very grave. "It frequently ends in disaster for the obsessed!"

Sergeant Reams chuckled. Kirkpatrick's lips twitched.

IN HIS car with Nita van Sloan, the Spider was garbed once

46

again as Richard Wentworth, man-about-town. He was smiling, but there was concern in his eyes. "I hope Kirkpatrick won't be too hard on the inspector," he said, "though Littlejohn was a fool to dash in alone like that. I tried to ease things for Littlejohn by making Kirkpatrick laugh."

Nita laughed softly. "Not that the inspector will appreciate your concern!"

Wentworth chuckled, "I imagine not!"

Twice before, his eyes had flicked to the special rear vision mirror in the tonneau of his limousine. Now he looked there again, shook his head.

"I actually believe that coupé—the one with the Oklahoma license—is following us, Nita," he said, "though it's the most inept bit of trailing I ever saw! The car stays not more than a half block behind us all the time, and at that last traffic light, it stopped in the middle of the block!"

Nita stared into the mirror, watching the car. "There's one man in the coupé," she said, and worry crept into her voice. "But, Dick, suppose he has been trailing for some time! Suppose, he saw you leave the car… as the Spider!"

Wentworth shook his head. "No, I have an idea it's the same man who took a pot shot at me in that basement! It will be easy to tell… I tear-gassed him!" Wentworth leaned forward and, at his orders, Ram Singh sent the limousine bounding forward. It whipped to the right, turned the corner a second time before the coupé was in sight… and moments later, it was just behind the coupé.

"Now," Wentworth said quietly, "crowd him to the curb!"

Ram Singh inched the big limousine over. The man's white face swung toward them, and a gun glinted in his right hand. Then fenders rasped together, and he caught the wheel fren-

ziedly, slammed on brakes. When the cars stopped, Wentworth was just opposite the driver.

He looked at the man calmly, through the panel of bullet-proof glass.

"Why, he's only a boy, Dick!" Nita cried.

Wentworth touched a button which flicked down the panel of bullet-proof glass. He leaned to the window.

"You were following me," he said quietly, "that was a foolish and dangerous thing to do."

The boy's face flushed, but his jaw was set stubbornly. "I reckon I'm not afraid of danger," he said, in a flat, Western drawl.

Wentworth studied him intently through a long moment. The boy was not more than twenty; his tanned face was honest, with its wide-set hazel eyes. The freckles across the bridge of his nose made him seem absurdly young. Wentworth smiled suddenly.

"I'm sure you're not afraid," he said quietly. "I'd like to talk to you, and since you aren't afraid, how about driving my car home for me? My man will bring yours right behind us."

Hesitation showed in the boy's eyes, "You're not making me do it," he said, shortly.

"Not at all," Wentworth assured him. "May I introduce myself? I am Richard Wentworth. This is Miss van Sloan."

The boy tugged off his soft hat. "I'm Jack Murdock," he said, and his eyes held intently on Wentworth's face as he spoke.

"Will you take the wheel, Mr. Murdock?" Wentworth asked gravely.

Ram Singh had truculence in his shoulders as he climbed out of the car. His eyes flashed darkly to Wentworth's face, and there was contempt in his manner as he got into the coupé. He wrenched the coupé out of its jam, slammed it forward with a clatter and roar. Nita smiled, but there was doubt in her eyes

as she watched Jack Murdock get in behind the wheel of the limousine.

"Dick, I don't understand," she said.

Wentworth shook his head, and there was a frown between his own eyes. "I'm not quite certain I do myself," he said. "I remember—" He cut off his words, to direct Murdock to his home. It wasn't really necessary, he saw, for without waiting for directions, Murdock had made the right turn!

NITA'S QUICK eyes, going to Wentworth's face, told that she, too, had recognized the meaning of that right turn. They did not talk after that, until Wentworth had ushered Jack Murdock into the drawing room of his Fifth Avenue penthouse.

Murdock's eyes went about him at the quietly luxurious furnishings and there was a belligerence and hostility in his bearing. He accepted a proffered cigarette with a short nod.

"You knew me, Mr. Murdock," he said quietly. "You knew where my home was. You were following me, because you did know me. Don't you think I'm entitled to know why?"

Murdock stood stiffly. His body was thin, wiry, and his clothing did not fit him too well. But he had a pride of bearing that made those things unimportant. His sandy hair stood up in wiry spikes. He set his jaw hard.

"Sure, I guess you are," he said slowly. "My father was Spain Murdock."

51

Wentworth's brows lifted politely. "Yes?" he said.

"My father was as square a man as ever lived!" the boy said, and defiance was in his voice. "He always treated me an' ma and the kids swell. He came to New York about five years ago on business."

Jack Murdock stopped and swallowed. Seated on the couch, Nita watched him with a dawning realization in her eyes. She busied herself with lighting a cigarette to hide the pain that touched her gentle mouth. But Dick's face showed only polite interest.

Jack Murdock's eyes blinked rapidly. They glistened. His voice turned angry.

"My father was killed here in New York," he said harshly. "He was shot through the forehead. A guy they call the Spider put a red thing on his forehead, right where he was shot!"

Wentworth said gravely, "I'm sorry to hear that, Mr. Murdock. Could I offer you something to drink?"

The boy shook his head sharply. "My dad never drank, and I ain't never going to, either!"

Wentworth gestured him toward a chair. His face was grave with sympathy. "I'm not going to pretend I don't understand your implication, Mr. Murdock," he said quietly. "Many men have… misunderstood my relation with the Spider. The police know that I have, on occasion, seen the Spider. They believe that I have ways of getting in contact with him when necessary. You found out about this some way—"

"My uncle's a Pink," Jack Murdock said, proudly. "He's one of the best men Pinkerton's got!"

52

Wentworth nodded, "So you thought you would follow me and find the Spider." He leaned forward. "Will you take a word of advice from me, Jack, a friendly word?"

The boy shook his head stubbornly. "I'm not going to give up!" he said. "Out where I come from, a fellow don't take a trail less'n he's going through with it. Me, I've taken the trail! I'm going to find this Spider, and when I do...."

Nita's hand crept out and rested on Wentworth's. Her eyes rested in warm sympathy on the boy.

Wentworth was frowning down at the tip of his cigarette. His left hand turned, clasped Nita's.

Jack Murdock's voice was still angry. "People tell me the Spider only kills crooks, but my dad wasn't a crook! He was a swell, square-shooting guy! Nobody can tell me nothing different, either!"

WENTWORTH LOOKED up, and he was smiling. "Nobody better say a thing like that where I can hear them, Mr. Murdock!" he said. "I wonder if I could make a bargain with you, Mr. Murdock?"

"I won't go away!"

Wentworth shook his head. "What I mean is this: If I should make contact with the Spider, I might be able to arrange for you to meet him for...."

Nita's hand tightened convulsively, "Dick!"

"...for a discussion," Wentworth went on. "After you talked with him, you might... make up your own mind."

Jack Murdock's freckles stood out strongly against his whitening face.

53

Wentworth continued earnestly. "In return, I would want your promise—on your honor—to stop this dangerous business of following people around—"

"Talking wouldn't do any good," the boy snapped. "Nobody's going to tell me my dad was a crook!"

Wentworth did not speak. He lifted a slow hand to his forehead and massaged the crease between his brows. There was an ache in his heart.

"Look," said the boy. "Look, Mr. Wentworth, I'm not making any promises about afterward, and nobody's going to talk me out of anything, but—well, a man ought to look another man in the eye and give him warning before he goes gunning for him!"

Wentworth nodded, "Yes, you're right, Mr. Murdock. Is it a deal, then?"

Jack Murdock grinned suddenly. "Yeah! Shake!" He stuck out his boy's hand, and the knuckles were grubby. Wentworth clasped it firmly, and his eyes were gravely smiling.

Jack Murdock's grin turned a little sheepish. "Gee, Mr. Wentworth," he said. "You're a swell guy! You—you remind me of—my dad!"

Wentworth said, "Thank you."

He meant it.

After he had taken the boy's address and shown him to the door, he came back to where Nita sat and now there was no dissembling in his face. Pain was in his eyes.

"Was it… a mistake, Dick?" she asked. "Do you remember?"

"Remember!" Wentworth laughed harshly, struck his chest with his fist. "Don't you know that the name of every man who ever died by my hand is carved here? They deserved death, every one of them. But their families, their parents...."

"But, Dick, you serve... *humanity!*"

WENTWORTH SWUNG aside to the doors that opened on the terrace, that showed the sparkling sky-line of the city he loved. He stood with rigidly braced shoulders and up-thrown head, his hands locked behind him. Nita did not follow, but sat upon the divan where he had left her. There was suffering in her eyes, too.

To no one in the world, save only her, did Dick Wentworth ever reveal this secret self. She knew the black despair, the doubts that shook him, whatever face he turned to the world. She knew, too, the toll that these secret sufferings took of the kindly man who had dedicated his life to the service of others!

When Dick came back to her, his lips were twisted in quizzical self-mockery, but his voice was steady. "Spain Murdock was not a big crook," he said, "and I didn't inquire into his motives, naturally. He organized a band of bank robbers, and I stumbled on their raid. He had just shot down a policeman... old Mike Littlejohn, the inspector's father. Spain Murdock almost got away. I followed and—killed him. I don't think the police ever connected him with the bank robbery. It didn't seem necessary for the Spider to explain."

Nita's hands reached out to Wentworth and she drew him to divan beside her, pulled his head down to her shoulder. "You mustn't torture yourself, Dick," she said. "The boy will have to be told."

Wentworth shook his head, "No, Nita, he must never be told!"

55

He sat bolt upright. "Do you think I'd have on my conscience the fact that I destroyed any boy's faith in his father! No, Nita, there must be another way!"

"But you're not going to meet him as the Spider," Nita said shortly. "I won't permit it! Oh, Dick, the boy seems entirely honest—I know he is—But criminals have used honest men for their own purposes before this! How do you know that crooks haven't set him on your trail? How do you know that, meeting him, the Spider won't walk into a death trap?"

Nita jumped to her feet, made an impatient circuit of the room. "Dick, you're not listening to me!" she stormed. "You've made up that stubborn mind of yours, and nothing is going to change you! Oh, Dick, I could—I could kiss you!"

Wentworth laughed and stood up to meet her. "All offerings gratefully received," he said.

IN THE street below, Jack Murdock climbed into his old car and swung it jubilantly out into the deserted avenue. He whistled between his teeth. He was new to the city. He didn't notice the car that, very skillfully, took his trail. It didn't stay in back of him. Sometimes it was ahead of him, sometimes beside him. And the two men in the car never seemed to look at Jack Murdock....

"Hell, Dropper," one grumbled, "I think the boss is nuts, making us trail this kid."

The other man shook a thin, hatchet face. His lips wore a perpetual smile. It was thin, and it drew his mouth corners back in small hard puckers in his cheeks.

"He got in to see Wentworth didn't he?" Dropper asked softly. "The boss is smart… This kid will lead us to the Spider!"

## CHAPTER 5
## DESIGN FOR DYING

WHEN RICHARD WENTWORTH strode briskly into police headquarters early next morning, he found Commissioner Kirkpatrick there before him. His friend was spruce as always… the inevitable gardenia was in a vase on his desk, ready for his lapel… but weariness had laid dark smudges beneath his keen angry eyes. It was plain that Kirkpatrick had been at work all night.

"We're getting nowhere on this case," he said curtly. "Dick, you'll have to work with me—and I want none of this vanishing at inopportune moments." He was smiling, but the expression was grim. "You're my charm against appearances of the Spider, Dick. Somehow, when you're with me, the man just doesn't show up!"

Wentworth agreed amiably. "If it's a good luck charm you want, Kirk, I can get a bonafide rabbit's foot for you… the left hind leg, shot at midnight, in a cemetery, on the night of All Hallow's Eve."

Kirkpatrick remained grim. "I'll get along with just you. There have been only two small developments during the night. I'm having the owner of the butcher shop chain brought in this morning, though he appears innocent…."

"A suspicious circumstance!" Wentworth jested.

57

Kirkpatrick's face began to relax. "So Inspector Littlejohn seems to think," he agreed. "But I've known Henry Schultz for a considerable while. He started out with a Yorkville shop, built it up, store by store. He's a thoroughly honest burgher of the old type."

"How about the manager of that particular shop?" Wentworth asked.

"He is dead!" Kirkpatrick said somberly. "It was Morris Bacon's brother!"

Wentworth lifted his brows, drew out his cigarette case. "I believe the last estimates put Morris Bacon's estate at about four and a half millions."

"He and his brother never got along well." Kirkpatrick leaned back, linked his fingers behind his head. "I've heard Morris declaim by the hour against what he called his brother's communistic leanings. Appeared to upset Morris that his brother wouldn't accept any of the Bacon money."

The annunciator signal whirred on Kirkpatrick's desk. He slapped down a cam, heard the voice of Cassidy from the outer office.

"Henry Schultz," the voice said, "with two lawyers."

Kirkpatrick's voice was impatient, "All right. Send them in."

The two lawyers convoyed Henry Schultz through the door. He looked exactly what he was, a prosperous butcher. His cheeks were florid from much red meat, and there were many scars on his ungloved hands. He thrust his big stomach, draped in a heavy double golden watch chain, comfortably before him. But his blue eyes were worried.

"I am sorry about this business, Mr. Kirkpatrick," he said, gutturally.

"Nonsense!" piped one lawyer. "You have nothing to be sorry about!"

The other lawyer, dapper and sharp, slapped his fingers on the edge of Kirkpatrick's desk. "This is an outrage. Mr. Schultz is a busy man! Yet you send for him like any two-bit punk."

Schultz said, irritably, "You must stop talking and give me my chance. Mr. Kirkpatrick, I did not want these two along, but my son insisted."

"He was right!" said one lawyer.

"Your rights must be protected, Mr. Schultz!" cried the other.

Schultz was like a St. Bernard dog badgered by terriers. He turned his head wearily toward each one of them in turn. They jabbered on. He struck his solid fist heavily on the desk.

"Shut up!" he bellowed. "Und get oud! Get oud, I tell you!"

HE SHOOED two lawyers out of the door, escorting them, protesting, to be sure they made their exits. Wentworth smiled faintly at Kirkpatrick.

"An impressive display of innocence," he said.

Kirkpatrick frowned and began snapping questions at Schultz. The butcher took his time with each answer. He seemed harassed and anxious to help. His eyes kept straying apologetically to Wentworth. In the end, Kirkpatrick dismissed him irritably, and the two attorneys began to yap outside the door. It was a relief when its closing shut off the sound.

The annunciator whirred again, "Mr. Morris Bacon insists on seeing you, sir," Cassidy reported. "Inspector Littlejohn wants to report an arrest he says is important. He's on his way in to headquarters now with the prisoner."

Kirkpatrick said, "Bacon in two minutes. Littlejohn when he arrives." He turned his eyes on Wentworth. "What do you think of Schultz?"

Wentworth leaned back in his chair. "He's worried about more than the torture business," he said. "And for some strange reason, he's particularly interested in me."

Kirkpatrick nodded. "My idea exactly. I'll have some further checking done on him... and his son." He depressed another cam on the annunciator, issued the order, and looked up as Morris Bacon was shown into the office. There was a girl with him, a girl with dark frightened eyes.

Bacon came to Kirkpatrick's desk with quick nervous strides, shook hands with a single hard pumping motion, jerked his head toward Wentworth.

"Wentworth!" he said, and shook hands the same way. His hand jerked toward the girl. "My daughter, Anne," he said.

Wentworth placed a chair for the girl and she smiled up at him, almost timidly. Morris Bacon set his hat precisely on the desk, brushed back his long, graying hair with a simultaneous drag of both hands. When he took the paper from his inner pocket it was with the quick gesture of a man drawing a gun in an emergency. He dropped it on the desk as if he hated it.

"Summons from a man calling himself Judge Torture," he said. "For Anne. 'Come prepared to pay two hundred thousand dollar fine,' it says."

Kirkpatrick caught up the paper, read it through swiftly. "This is fantastic," he said. "Miss Bacon is summoned to the home of Phideas McMann!"

He slapped down a cam on the box. "Get Phideas McMann on the phone," he ordered.

Cassidy's voice came in matter-of-factly. "Just about to ring you, Commissioner. Mr. McMann is here; wants to see you at once."

Wentworth's gray-blue eyes were keen with thought. He knew McMann more by reputation than by sight. One of the world's wealthiest bankers, it was strange that he himself came to headquarters. Governors would come to his home at his bidding, and be flattered!

Phideas McMann came in quietly. He was a solid man who gave an impression of compact power. His face was clean-shaven, his jaw firm and long. His sharp dark eyes darted to each person in the room for a deliberate second before he spoke, then rested on the paper on Kirkpatrick's desk.

"You, too, Morris?" he asked Bacon.

"Anne!" Bacon snapped at him. "Utter nonsense. Summoned to your house at midnight—by Judge Torture!"

McMANN'S LIPS were a straight-cut across his face. "I don't doubt it," he said flatly. "Commissioner, I came to you

61

because it is apparent I can no longer trust my own guards, or employees, or even my own telephone!" He deliberately drew out a similar legal summons, placed it carefully on the desk. "I am summoned at midnight, in my own home. It is specified that at this hour I must be in my clock room, and the summons calls my attention to the 'displeasure' of Judge Torture exhibited in a certain butcher shop last night. The paper was placed in my pajama jacket during the night—and I spend fifty thousand a year to guard my estate!"

Kirkpatrick rose to his feet, his eyes sharp and the weariness gone from his face. "I'll place my best men with you today, Mr. McMann," he said quietly. "I'll be at your estate tonight myself."

McMann eyed Kirkpatrick keenly for a moment, nodded crisply. "I'll leave the details to you, Commissioner. Anything you want or need, ask for it!"

He strode toward the office door, but halted as it was batted open from outside. Inspector Littlejohn thrust a prisoner into the office, handcuffs glittering on his wrists, and Wentworth tensed.

"This man," said Littlejohn harshly, "works for Judge Torture!"

The prisoner was—Jack Murdock!

**PHIDEAS McMANN** hesitated a moment, then nodded to Kirkpatrick and strode out. Inspector Littlejohn thrust the boy forward, and Littlejohn's eyes were hot and excited.

"Last night," he said, "I happened to notice near the Frisco Club, a car with an Oklahoma license on it. Today, I see the same car near Schultz's place... where we found the tortured men last night. And I see the bulge on his hip where he carries a gun. I

shook him down and—"he tossed a gun to Kirkpatrick's desk—
"It's the automatic Mr. Wentworth reported stolen. I've already
had ballistics tests made. A bullet from this gun killed Briscoe!"

Wentworth felt a sharp constriction of his heart. His brain
became cold and crystal clear. No matter what happened now,
Wentworth was in serious danger. If the boy told the truth about
the gun, it was almost certain that he would accuse Wentworth
of being the Spider! If he did not, he faced a murder rap… and
Wentworth could not stand by idly and allow Murdock to suffer!

While the thought raced through his brain, Wentworth
stepped forward to the desk. "This is rather foolish, Kirk," he said
quietly. "Mr. Murdock had nothing to do with killing Briscoe,
and I'll take an oath to it!"

Jack Murdock's head was flung up defiantly. When Wentworth spoke, he looked quickly at him… and a slow grin came
to his lips.

"Thanks, Mr. Wentworth," he said. "I didn't expect to have a
friend here!"

Kirkpatrick snapped a quick question at Wentworth, but
Wentworth shook his head. "Let's hear the rest of Littlejohn's
story," he said. "I see that Mr. Murdock's head has been injured.
Littlejohn must have learned something—" his voice became
angry, and brittle—"if only that you don't get answers from boys
like Jack Murdock by beating them up!"

Littlejohn's cheekbones spotted with anger. Kirkpatrick was
abruptly on his feet, and Morris Bacon cowered in the background. Wentworth saw Anne Bacon's eyes, dark with sympathy,

rest on Jack Murdock; saw Jack Murdock look at her. After that, the boy seemed unable to take eyes off the girl.

"Littlejohn," Kirkpatrick's voice rasped, "you know my orders on such tactics!"

The inspector fairly spat out words. "I could show a mark or two myself!" he said. "What do you think I put handcuffs on him for?"

Wentworth grinned suddenly, "Don't tell me, Mr. Murdock, that you resisted arrest?"

Murdock grinned, and it wrinkled his freckled nose. "Well, now, Mr. Wentworth," he said. "How did I know he was a cop? A guy can lie about being a cop. I didn't like the way he started searching me right off."

Kirkpatrick's jaw was grim. "Do you want to make any complaint," he demanded, "before you begin your explanations?"

Jack Murdock felt the authority in Kirkpatrick's voice. His head swung about, though once more his eyes trailed across the sympathetic face of Anne Bacon. "No complaints, sir," he said quietly. "I did resist arrest. I guess I gave almost as good as I got. And I did have a gun. You might say I stole it... but I haven't killed anybody with it. And I don't work for Judge Torture or any other man! I came here—" he glanced toward Wentworth, and shut his lips tightly. "That's the story, sir."

Littlejohn said angrily, "I can't get a word of explanation or anything else out of him!"

Wentworth said, "May I suggest, Kirkpatrick, that a man should be treated as a man, and not as a child? I'm sure that

Murdock will answer any reasonable question, put to him in a decent way. You can't bully Oklahoma boys like this one."

Littlejohn swung toward Wentworth. "Why don't you just take over the Commissioner's job, Wentworth?" he snapped. "I'm sure you could do much better!"

WENTWORTH ALLOWED a faint smile to move his lips, but his voice was grave. "Kirk, I believe I did overstep proper bounds. I apologize to you. I seem to have an unfortunate way of, shall we say, getting in the hair of Inspector Littlejohn." His voice took on an edge. "But I detest bullies in uniform!"

"That will do," Kirkpatrick said sharply. "Dick, you're here because I asked your help, though your position is anomalous. However, you're definitely out of order. Inspector, let there be an end of this baiting. Take the cuffs off Murdock."

Inspector Littlejohn flushed under the rebuke, but his face was utterly stolid as he unlocked the handcuffs from Murdock's wrists. Murdock disdained to massage them, stood very straight.

"Thank you, sir," he said. "I'll be glad to tell *you* what I know." He turned toward Wentworth apologetically. "If you don't object, sir?"

Wentworth shook his head, aware of the suspicious glare of Inspector Littlejohn. Murdock seemed suddenly embarrassed, but he braced his shoulders and his eyes were defiant.

"My dad was a swell guy," he said. "He never did a crooked thing in his life. He was Spain Murdock. Five years ago the Spider killed him here in New York and put that nasty seal on his forehead."

65

Kirkpatrick suppressed an exclamation, clasped his hands on the desk. "Go ahead. Murdock," he said.

"Yes, sir," the boy said. "I've got an uncle who is a Pinkerton man. My mother's brother. He had a sort of idea Mr. Wentworth might lead me to the Spider on account of they show up on the same cases lots of times. I—followed Mr. Wentworth to the Frisco club last night."

Kirkpatrick's eyes shifted to Wentworth through a long minute. Littlejohn's eyes were avid, and Morris Bacon cleared his throat. "Frisco Club," he said nervously. "The Spider killed a man there, didn't he?"

No one answered him. Littlejohn snapped out a question. "Did Wentworth go there alone or with a woman?"

Wentworth stiffened. Littlejohn's manner of speech was insulting, but Murdock was answering stiffly.

"I followed his car, and I didn't see him go inside," he said. "I got caught on a traffic light."

Wentworth had difficulty in suppressing a breath of relief, but his automatic, lying on the desk, was a brilliant point of danger. Murdock had said, *"You might say I stole the gun..."* But that gun had disappeared from Briscoe's office while Richard Wentworth was imprinting the seal of the Spider upon the forehead of a dead man! *What had Murdock seen?*

Kirkpatrick was tense on the edge of his chair. He said, quietly, "Go on, Murdock."

Murdock shifted his footing a little. He looked Kirkpatrick directly in the eye. "I guess what I did wasn't strictly according to Hoyle, Mr. Kirkpatrick," he said.

Kirkpatrick interrupted, "Wait just a minute. Let me get this straight. Do I understand that you actually came to New York with the idea of... finding the Spider... and avenging your father's murder?" His voice was incredulous.

Murdock's jaw grew stubborn. "The Spider's a crook. There's rewards for him. Anybody's got the right to hunt for him."

Kirkpatrick said sharply, "That's not the point, Murdock! You don't seem to realize that the Spider is one of the most deadly criminals that ever lived! Even I don't know how many men he has killed!"

Murdock merely said, "Anybody's got the right to hunt him. And he killed my dad."

Littlejohn snorted. "He's lying! He's one of Judge Torture's men!"

Murdock swung around. "No man can call me a liar," he said, his voice quivering. "You either take that back, or I'll try to knock your head off."

LITTLEJOHN'S FACE went blank. A slow smile stirred Kirkpatrick's lips. "Mr. Murdock, I apologize for the inspector," he said, "but the truth is that, around here, we aren't used to people who tell the truth. It's a bit of a surprise. Would you go on with what happened last night?"

The boy turned back reluctantly toward Kirkpatrick. "Okay," he muttered. "Look, Mr. Kirkpatrick, I give you my word of honor—"

"I accept it," Kirkpatrick said quietly and sincerely.

Wentworth, even in the tension of waiting for the boy to continue, could not help but see how completely Kirkpatrick

67

gauged Murdock. It was precisely this quality of misunderstanding which made him the great commissioner he was. There wasn't a man on the force, including the difficult Littlejohn, who wouldn't lay his life on the line for Commissioner Stanley Kirkpatrick.

Murdock relaxed. "Thanks," he said. "Well, I saw that Mr. Wentworth's car was parked near, so I tried to get in the club, but they didn't like my clothes. I went down the alley and there was a fire escape there. I climbed up it, thinking maybe I could get a slant at Mr. Wentworth. When I was on my way up, somebody shot off a gun. I couldn't hear it very well, but there was a window up there. I sort of eased it up."

Wentworth's eyes were veiled. No doubt now that the boy had seen him implant the seal! The timing could not have been more perfect. But if that was true why had not the boy made some attempt on his life? Wentworth glanced swiftly about the room. He realized that there was a strong chance he would have to make a break for liberty!

He was prepared at any time to disappear completely as Richard Wentworth, for this threat of identification as the Spider must always hang over his head. He was completely cool, unexcited. His mind had already canvassed the possibilities. If Murdock made his identification, he was finished as Richard Wentworth. It was the one accusation he could not fight... not against an honest man!

Wentworth realized that Littlejohn had dropped back a stride and had stealthily drawn his revolver!

"You were looking into Briscoe's office," Kirkpatrick said

softly. "In that room, two men were killed, and one of them had the seal of the Spider on his forehead. The seal of the man who killed your father! Murdock, what did you see?"

Murdock was frowning. He glanced toward Wentworth, and his eyes came back to Kirkpatrick, puzzled.

"A man has to be awful careful at a time like this," he said. "A man's life is at stake, and you can't make any mistakes at a time like that."

Kirkpatrick said quietly, "I'm sure you won't make any mistake, Murdock. I'm also sure you won't lie to me for any reason whatever."

Murdock's jaw set. "No, sir, I won't!" he said. "I looked in this window and I saw a man reach down and press something metal against the forehead of a fellow in a funny sort of coat. When he stood up, the Spider's seal was on the man's forehead. I didn't have a gun—my uncle took mine away—but there was one on the floor just under the window. I reached in and picked it up."

MURDOCK SWALLOWED. His fists were in knots at his side. Wentworth deliberately took out a cigarette, and tucked it between his lips. He took out his cigarette lighter, flicked it, but he didn't touch flame to the cigarette. For if he did, the room would fill with stinking black smoke. Littlejohn wasn't looking at the boy at all, but at Wentworth.

"Well, there he was," said Murdock thickly, "the man who had killed my dad. I had a gun in my hand, and I knew how to use it… I couldn't shoot him in the back, of course. But all I had to do was sing out and tell him to turn around and fill his hand. It would be an even chance."

69

Kirkpatrick's eyes held an incredulous light. He said, "For God's sake, son—"

Murdock's jaw looked stubborn. "I know. My uncle told me. You can't even see the Spider's hand when he draws, it's so fast. But it had to be that way or not at all. And I wasn't afraid. After all, I had right on my side."

Kirkpatrick's tension softened. Wentworth felt something hard in his throat that made his breathing a little difficult. In this world and age to find a man who could still believe that right and justice must triumph through divine intervention of Providence!

"I wasn't afraid," Murdock was repeating, in a puzzled tone of voice, "but somehow I didn't call out to the Spider. That's a funny thing. I've been thinking a lot about it ever since. There he was, there was a gun in my hand—and he had killed my dad. But I didn't call out to him. Why?"

Kirkpatrick's fingers interlaced. The knuckles were white. "There is no longer any doubt in my mind, son," he said, "that every word of your story is true. You saw the Spider. As to why you didn't shoot, I can't answer that. But I can tell you this: There have been many men who have followed the Spider. They have called him… Master of Men!"

Murdock said, slowly, "Master of Men? Well, I didn't shoot. Instead, I ducked back out of the window, ran around and locked the door of the office. I put through a call to the police on a phone in the washroom, and then I went back outside. I saw somebody at the window a little while later, and put a bullet through the glass."

70

Kirkpatrick interrupted him, "Wait a minute, Murdock. Go back with me now to the fire escape. Look into the room. What did the Spider look like?"

Murdock nodded. "He had on a tailcoat. He had black hair. I don't know just how tall he was."

Littlejohn said harshly, "The truth, Murdock! It was Wentworth, wasn't it?"

Murdock's face was pale. "That's just it, sir. I can't make a mistake now, Mr. Kirkpatrick. I followed Mr. Wentworth home afterward. He saw me, asked me up to his place. I talked to him, as close as I am to you now, sir."

"Quit stalling!" Littlejohn snapped.

"But don't you see, sir," Murdock appealed to Kirkpatrick. "When a man is standing straight, he looks different from the way he would when his *shoulders are humped up like a hunchback!*"

WENTWORTH KNEW that a sharp breath escaped him, and once more he didn't light the cigarette. He snapped out the flame and stared at Murdock. His shoulders… *hunched?* It was true that when he wore the disguise of the Spider, he assumed that twisted shape to conceal his true figure and carriage. But this night, it had been Wentworth, not the Spider, who stooped to place the seal on the dead man's forehead!

Kirkpatrick was snapping sharp questions at Murdock; Littlejohn was at the door with his gun in his fist. But Wentworth threw his mind back to that scene in Briscoe's office. And he could not remember. Was Murdock lying now, protecting Wentworth for his own personal vengeance? Or was he telling the truth?

71

Had Wentworth, stooping to implant that seal as he had so many times before, *subconsciously* hunched his body into the menacing crouch of the Spider? Somehow, the thought terrified Wentworth a little, even when it brought him the assurance of safety, temporarily. Where did Richard Wentworth cease as an individual... and the Spider begin? Could any man live those two separate lives and keep them in different compartments of his brain, of his soul?

Wentworth knew suddenly that the boy spoke the literal truth. Imprinting that seal, Wentworth had become—for the moment—*the Spider!*

The sharp voice of Kirkpatrick aroused him. "Dick, we'll settle this once and for all right now. You've at least seen the Spider. Turn your back, hunch your shoulders and stoop over to the floor. You have your cigarette lighter in your hand. You will imagine that you are using that lighter... *to print the seal of the Spider on the forehead of a dead man!*"

## CHAPTER 6
## COURT CONVENES

FOR AN instant Wentworth stared incredulously at Kirkpatrick, then he forced an easy laugh.

"I gather that Littlejohn has converted you to the ranks of suspicion, Kirk," he said. "I'll submit, of course, though I scarcely think it a fair test. As you say, I've seen the Spider, and I am a pretty fair imitator. If I do a good job, I'll probably be executed as the Spider. If I do a bad job, I'll be more under suspicion than ever. However...."

Wentworth started to turn his back toward the others, but it was Kirkpatrick who called a halt. "You're quite right, Dick," he said. "It wouldn't be a fair test!"

Wentworth shrugged, twisted his shoulders and deliberately stooped over. He faced a task of extraordinary difficulty. He must give a fair imitation—yet disguise the crouch!

Murdock said, "I don't believe Mr. Wentworth is the Spider anyway. He treated me white. A square guy like him wouldn't kill an innocent man."

Littlejohn said, "To hell with this posie-to sing. Wentworth lost his gun; you found it in the murder room. Take a look at him crouching there and tell me just one thing: Does he look like the Spider—or not!"

Young Murdock looked long at the stooped, hunched figure of Richard Wentworth. At last he said, "It's too important for me to make a mistake... In a way—he looks like the man I saw. Yet I don't believe he is."

Wentworth stood up, relaxed. He laughed. "Really, my dear inspector," he said. "I've never heard such prompting of a witness! I've told you that I carried the gun in my car... that it was stolen. You know yourself that I wore no gun holster when you searched me a short while afterward." He shook his head. "Now, to make the test complete, Inspector Littlejohn, you should pose for us as... Judge Torture!"

KIRKPATRICK'S VOICE cut through crisply as Littlejohn started a furious protest. "The test was unfair," he said. "I

73

The thing that appended from the great clock was—it *had been*—a human being!

acknowledge that. Murdock, I don't want to be hard on you. I could hold you on a charge of possessing this gun. I would rather hold you as a material witness."

Wentworth smiled. "In that way, Murdock, if they want to use you as a witness, your testimony won't be prejudiced by a gun-carrier's record."

Kirkpatrick flushed, but made no answer. Murdock shrugged. "If you got to put me in jail, it doesn't matter to me what the charge is—short of murder," he said. "But look, Mr. Kirkpatrick, you're a white guy. Don't hold me there long. You see, I've got a job to do."

He smiled hesitantly at Wentworth, held out his hand. "No hard feelings, sir?"

Wentworth gripped his hand warmly. "No hard feelings at all, Murdock. I'd offer to help you, but the watchdogs might consider it an effort to prejudice a witness."

When the boy had been taken away by Inspector Littlejohn, Kirkpatrick faced Morris Bacon and his daughter, who were still in the room.

"I'm sorry for the interruption, Mr. Bacon," he said formally. "I want to post a police guard over you and your daughter. I think it will be best if you go to Mr. McMann's tonight. I'll arrange for transportation."

Bacon came to the desk. "I didn't have time to tell you," he said. "My brother… last night. I didn't get along with him, but he was still my brother! Bonds of blood, you know. He was murdered horribly."

Kirkpatrick said, "I know, Mr. Bacon. He was identified without calling you in. You have my sincerest sympathy."

Bacon's face was lined. "My brother," he said. "Now my daughter is threatened."

Kirkpatrick's hand dropped on Bacon's shoulder. "We'll protect you!" he promised grimly.

Anne Bacon offered her hand, shyly. "Don't be too hard on that young man," she said, gently. "I'm sure he was trying very hard to be fair and honest."

Kirkpatrick nodded curtly. "He was, without a doubt. My men will watch over you. Tonight, I'll take over the job!" His jaw grew grim. "Tonight, we'll stop Judge Torture!"

## JUDGEMENT OF THE DAMNED

THERE WAS an almost hysterical gaiety that night in the elaborate home of Phideas McMann. He had spread an austerely beautiful table in the museum-like hall to which the summons of Judge Torture had called them. The walls were alive with the flicking pendulums of a thousand clocks that hung there; the room was murmurous with their voices. It was in this company that the party of six sat down to a late dinner: the intended victims of Judge Torture, and their guards.

It had been after eleven when they came to this room, and since that time the doors had not been opened. Commissioner Kirkpatrick had stipulated that service must be entirely from within the room; the entrances had been locked and, both inside and outside of every window and door, stood grim-faced police. The grounds of the estate were patrolled by men on foot, and radio cars... a full hundred police had been assigned to the task. Yet there was an overtone of shrillness in the laughter around the table. As the hour of midnight drew near, eyes strayed again and again to the myriad clocks that whispered away the seconds as though no menace existed.

Wentworth sat near the foot of the table, opposite Nita van Sloan. His eyes swept slowly over the faces of the other five guests. Anne Bacon, on the right hand of McMann, sat with her hands locked in her lap. Her laughter came at infrequent intervals, and it was sharp and strained. Morris Bacon himself fiddled nervously with his wine glass. Even Kirkpatrick was jerky in his movement. Of them all, Phideas McMann seemed least disturbed. He was explaining about a single clock which filled an entire end of the room.

"One of the most famous clocks in the world," he said. "One of the greatest Flemish clock makers spent his entire lifetime building it."

Wentworth let his eyes flick toward the massive dial, around which the entire room had been built. Its hands stood at three minutes before midnight. The housing was an elaborate representation of a biblical scene, and there were doorways over which angelic cherubs spread their wings.

"Upon the stroke of twelve," McMann was explaining to Anne Bacon, "the central door over the dial opens, and a life-size figure of a priest comes out to pronounce a blessing with uplifted hand. At the same time, there is a parade of the twelve apostles. They march out of the door on the left and disappear through the door of the right. During their parade, the carillon of the clock tolls out a *Te Deum*. It is really quite impressive."

Anne Bacon laughed. "And at the same time, all these other clocks are going to strike! It must be one awful bedlam."

"At the very least, bedlam," McMann chuckled. "It takes three men, working full time, to make sure that they all keep perfect time and strike together. This room is especially air-conditioned, kept at constant temperature and humidity winter and summer."

Wentworth turned to Kirkpatrick, who sat at the foot of the table. "Air-conditioners are perfect for gas attacks," he said quietly.

Kirkpatrick frowned. "I have three men stationed at the equipment," he said, "and it was thoroughly searched before they took their posts. McMann refused to cut it off entirely."

Wentworth lifted his brows. "Refused?" he murmured.

78

# JUDGEMENT OF THE DAMNED

In an instant, two of the executioners were twitching out their lives on the floor.

Kirkpatrick's gesture was curt. "Said it would ruin the clocks."
NITA LEANED toward Wentworth across the table. "Why
do you think Judge Torture specified this room?" she asked.
"Because of the clocks building up suspense?"

Wentworth shrugged slightly. There was silence in the hall
save for the whispering of the clocks. It increased in volume until
the ticking, rustling, murmuring seemed to be in the very head
of each person in the room. There was a clicking and whirring
as the strikers set for the strokes of twelve.

Wentworth's eyes concentrated on the Clock of the Apostles,
and Nita's words remained in his mind. Every watchman on the
premises was tense, expectant.

Wentworth came slowly to his feet. "The big clock, Kirk," he
said softly. "Those doors are large enough for men. There will be
a rear entrance, so that workmen can gain access to the machinery of the clock!"

Kirkpatrick snapped erect. "Right, Dick!" he agreed, and
strode toward the door to warn his men.

Wentworth shifted slightly in his seat. He had not wanted to
attend this dinner tonight, since his presence here thwarted his
plan to block an attack. But Kirk had been insistent; his suspicions had been re-aroused by Inspector Littlejohn, and by Jack
Murdock's story. Wentworth's lips smiled a little at memory of
the boy, and his eyes shifted to Anne Bacon where she sat beside
McMann and across the table from Morris Bacon.

She sat perfectly still, her gaze fastened on the clock. The great
minute hand had closed all save the last gap before midnight.

Even McMann's deep, penetrating voice had become silent. Bacon twisted about in his seat to stare at the big clock.

Swiftly, Wentworth's mind raced over the inspection trip he had made over the house. There was guards on the fuse boxes, and all main switches so that lights should not be thrown out. Every possible point of precaution was guarded. He peered out the window; floodlights picked out the trees, etched them against the black sky. Sound of the sentinels hailing each other, came from darkness off to the right, floated from man to man past the windows and died out off to the left. There was no break in the number hails.

Far off in the high reaches of the room, there was a faint snap, and a cuckoo clock piped its curious note. All over the room there was a whirring of a thousand tiny motors, and bedlam commenced. Anne Bacon began to laugh, thinly. Nita rose and moved toward her.

Wentworth did not stand, but he moved his shoulders to loosen his coat. His gun butts were clear beneath his arms. A thousand bell notes were tinkling, bonging, clanging. Westminster chimes pealed out, sonorous and deep. But all of these multitudinous notes were beaten into background as the great carillon of the Clock of the Apostles began to toll.

ON THE fourth note, the door above the dial swung out, and the priest moved forth, his hand lifted in benediction—and Wentworth's twin guns leaped to his hands!

McMann shouted and leapt to his feet, his chair crashing to the floor. Police guns blasted near the windows… but Wentworth held his fire.

81

He saw the figure of the priest jerk and quiver to the hammer of police lead… but it was only a figure.

It was a jest of Judge Torture… for the figure of the priest was robed in scarlet and wore the white wig of an English jurist. Atop the wig was the cap which early judges donned—to pronounce the sentence of death!

Kirkpatrick uttered commands and the hammer of guns stilled. McMann was swearing furiously over the damage to his clock. That was the situation when the last of the clocks tinkled into silence—all save the great Clock of the Apostles, which had just finished its preliminary *Te Deum*.

Now, the door at the left of the clock swung open, and the first of the apostles glided slowly forward to the timing of the first great bell stroke.

Wentworth heard Bacon's voice break out thinly. "Ridiculous!" he snapped. "Does this Judge Torture think he can frighten us with an effigy?"

Wentworth said quietly, "The clock hasn't finished striking."

The great clock struck the fourth time, and the first of the apostles glided back into the interior again. Wentworth let his eyes skip rapidly over the room. The police were at their posts again, white-faced with the strain. Their guns were in their fists. Bacon had his arm around Anne's shoulder.

As the clock struck the sixth time, the lights blacked out.

"Flashlights!" Wentworth snapped.

Before the darkness could start panic, the police had their flashlights blazing. The beams crossed and criss-crossed through the room, quested as restlessly as anti-aircraft batteries. Light bathed the face of the big clock. It was two seconds before Wentworth realized that this was not a result of the police lights. A powerful spot had been focused on it from the wall above the window.

"Just take it easy," Wentworth whispered softly. "All this is intended to start a panic so that the men of Judge Torture can strike! There is more coming… Kirk, the wires must have been severed outside of the estate! All inside points are guarded."

Kirkpatrick assented. The clock was striking the ninth time… and Wentworth was aware of Nita beside him.

"Dick," she said. "I smell something burning!"

Wentworth swore softly, and his flaring nostrils recorded the hot fumes of burning wood and cloth, hot metal. That meant a fire-bomb had been rigged somewhere here, set to go off when the electric wires were severed.

"Tell Kirkpatrick," he whispered to Nita. "I suggest that a solid phalanx of police be formed, to take the threatened people in its midst. When midnight is safely past, we can pass out of the room."

HIS EYES were riveted on the clock. That focused light meant the final blow would come from there. Even if it were intended only to divert attention from some other source of attack, something else threatened from that point. Wentworth's guns felt cold in his fists. Kirkpatrick was talking steadily, making arrangements for the exit. McMann's voice lifted in thick, furious curses.

"This isn't possible," he said fiercely. "The house is completely surrounded by the police, and yet—"

"These things could have been arranged before the police came," Wentworth said. "Quiet now!"

The eleventh apostle had made his exit from the left side of the clock. The twelfth was already a shadow in the doorway. Wentworth was aware that the fumes were thickening in the room. Thin spirals of blue smoke swirled across the nervous fingers of flashlights, lifted like incense toward the clock.

At that moment, the priest with his uplifted hand, the priest clad in robes of scarlet and with the cap of doom upon its head, began to speak!

The voice came from the figure. There could be no question of that. But the voice was the same that had whispered in the office before Briscoe had died... the voice of Judge Torture.

*"It is the judgment of this court,"* came the hissing, mocking voice, *"that you, Phideas McMann, shall be broken upon the sign of the thing you worship, and shall hang there until you are dead, dead... dead! May no deity have mercy on your soul!"*

Wentworth opened his lips to calm the hysterical cries that broke out, and a tearing scream split the darkness. For the twelfth apostle had made his exit into the bright beam of the spotlight and the sentence of Judge Torture was instantly clear!

For the twelfth apostle was not a figure like the rest. It was—it had been—a human being. His body had been horribly broken and twisted until it formed a crude *S*. One leg had been amputated at the thigh, and nailed across the body, so that it formed a ghastly, incredibly horrible dollar mark!

McMann's cry lifted hoarse and terrible in the murk of the

room. "No, no! Not that!" he screamed. "I'll pay! *I'll pay... Judge Torture!*"

Anne Bacon was screaming without ceasing. Kirkpatrick's voice lifted sharply. "No one leaves this room! Stand firm at the doors, men!"

The horribly dead body of the victim was gliding toward the exit on the far side of the platform. The robed scarlet figure representing Judge Torture was turning to retreat behind the door, and the last note of midnight had sounded and died.

Wentworth cried a warning to the police and sprinted across the room. He thrust his guns into their holsters as he ran, bounded high into the air—and clamped his hands on the edge of the platform where the apostles paraded! In an instant, he had flung himself after the final retreating figure. He cleared the door, and it swung shut!

FROM SOMEWHERE in the room, there was laughter, whispering, ugly laughter. The flashlights of the police quested for the sound and did not find its author. The spotlight that had focused on the clock went black.

Within the huge clock, Wentworth was aware of the whir of machinery, could feel the vibration of the great pendulum's swing. He flicked his flashlight and focused it on the figures of the apostles. The effigy which the tortured man had replaced lay discarded on the floor. The apostles had taken their appointed places, ready for their next parade.

Wentworth focused his light upon the last, gruesome figure, shaped horribly into a dollar mark. Wentworth's face was drawn thin and stern; his mouth was a bitter line. But the flash in his hand did not tremble. He laid it upon the face of the dead man, nodded crisply. He crossed to the body and tried to manipulate the jaw. It was locked fast by *rigor mortis*. He tried a leg… and it was limp.

Then Wentworth strode back to the exit door of the clock, swung it open and stepped out on the platform. Instantly, flashlights converged upon him. By their reflection, he could see that the panic-stricken prisoners had been surrounded by the police. A solid phalanx was formed about them… and it was time. The thick, swirling smoke of the room was all about them. High up where Wentworth stood, it was almost impossible to breathe. He swung to the floor, strode toward Kirkpatrick.

"According to *rigor mortis*," Wentworth said quietly, "the man has been dead from two to six hours. His jaw is stiff, his legs have not yet stiffened."

In the darkness, a woman sobbed softly. The doors were swung wide. Flashlights illuminated their path brilliantly. Awkwardly, the thick group of blue-uniformed men and the three threatened persons in their midst moved toward the front door of the home. McMann walked like a drunken man. His feet stumbled. Morris Bacon was shaking with fear. It was Anne who had sobbed.

Wentworth felt Nita's hand on his arm. Her voice reached no farther than his ear, "I recognized the dead man," she said. "It was one of those three who tortured the girl at the Frisco Club."

Wentworth nodded curtly. It was necessary to talk softly, for he could not admit that he had seen those three in the club. It had happened before he was supposed to have arrived!

But he was puzzled. He was positive the man had died more

than twenty-four hours ago… yet the signs of *rigor mortis* indicated a very much later death than that!

He lifted his voice: "Kirk, I don't think this is over yet! Warn your men to be doubly alert!"

The front doors swung open, and the slow-moving phalanx filed out upon the gravel driveway, moved toward the lawn beyond. Black smoke was billowing out of basement windows. Other police were already at work to curb the blaze.

The phalanx moved to the middle of the lawn, seventy-five feet from house or trees. It was there when the roar of an automobile engine hammered upon their ears. Wentworth whipped toward the sound, heard a man shout… and then the car was in sight! It was already rolling at terrific speed, and it was headed straight for the congested ranks of police and prisoners!

In a breath of time, the tight guard of police was broken! Men hurled themselves frantically aside, got in each other's way, fought furiously. Wentworth caught Nita from the rear ranks of the crowd, threw her over his shoulder and ran from the path of the car. He had recognized it now. Kirkpatrick's official car! EVEN AS he spotted it, the siren ripped wide open, and its shriek added to the wild confusion of the night. The headlights blazed out. In their glare Wentworth saw McMann racing for the trees; saw Bacon with Anne in his arms, stumble after McMann.

"After them!" Wentworth cried. "Kirk, watch those three!"

Kirkpatrick, he saw then, was prone upon the ground in the path of the car!

In the struggle to escape, he had tripped, struck his head!

Wentworth saw him stir feebly, try to rise, slip flat upon the ground again!

Horror lined Wentworth's throat with brass. He whirled about, Nita still on his shoulder, gun in his hand. Not a chance in the world of reaching Kirkpatrick in time to save him. There was just one chance—and Wentworth took it in the same split-second that he grasped the picture.

His gun spat in his right hand—blasted out the right front tire of the car! The car swerved and headed straight for him.

But Wentworth stood firm, the gun lifted in his hand. He could see the white face of the man behind the wheel as a menacing blur behind the windshield—but that windshield was bullet-proof as he well knew. Swiftly, Wentworth calculated his chances. He had deliberately turned the car toward himself, because it was the only chance to pull it aside from its straight course toward Kirkpatrick.

Unable to help, Nita did the only thing she could. She lay motionless and waited Wentworth's decision. His eyes were keen on the racing car, narrowed against the assault of the headlights. The driver was fighting the wheel, obviously trying to hold it steadily on Wentworth.

Wentworth, gun ready in his fist, still waited. He wanted to delay until his shot should be the determining factor. When he changed the balance on that steering wheel, as he intended to do, there must be no time for the killer to rectify it!

Wentworth waited… and the car was no more than thirty feet away when he fired! Instantly, the left front tire blew. The man's strength was all bent in twisting the wheel to the left against the savage pull of his right flat tire. Wentworth's bullet did the rest. The car slewed violently about to the right. Its rear end skidded wildly on the grass… and Wentworth flung himself in a frantic leap.

Wentworth's feet slipped on the grass. He felt himself falling, saw the black juggernaut of the car's rear sweep toward him. Falling, he doubled and twisted. He threw Nita from him to safety, hit rolling. There was a violent gush of air. His coat caught, and ripped. He was jerked sideways… and then the cloth tore, and the death car had swept past.

As Wentworth struck the ground, he heard a fusillade of gunfire split the night. A man's scream lifted, muffled. The big car slammed into a tree. There was a scream of torn metal, the jangle of broken glass. The tree tottered, its branches threshing. Inside the car, the man still screamed. But the tree was falling toward the car. Grandly, majestically, its high branches whining with speed, it swept downward. It struck, with a renewed clangor of steel, and after that, there was no more screaming.

WENTWORTH STAGGERED to his feet. "Stay with Kirkpatrick!" he cried to Nita. Then he sprinted toward the trees where McMann and Bacon and Anne had disappeared.

Wentworth was reeling as he ran. His breath was hot in his lungs, and his head was whirling. The car, catching him that glancing blow, had administered a heavy shock. It would not stop Wentworth. But it had shaken him, and his vision was not clear.

He shouted as he ran, shouted the names of the threatened three. He was bitterly angry. For all his careful planning, despite the heavy guard thrown around the place, Judge Torture had smashed the cordon... and gained at least an opportunity to strike at the three. Part of his fury was at Kirkpatrick, and part at himself. Had the Spider been free to roam the darkness tonight, he was certain he could have prevented this fiasco. Now, he could only try frantically to catch up the loose ends.

Into the darkness of the trees he plunged at full speed. He hurdled a bush, swerved past a tree, slanting the beam of his flashlight ahead. He caught a flash of red, heard a woman's cry... and sped toward the sound.

"It's Wentworth," he called. "Don't be frightened, Anne!"

He saw the girl try to run, too terrified to understand his words. He leaped after her and caught a fraction of a word shouted back to him. *"... dang...."*

Even as he recognized her cry of danger and tried to dodge, he caught movement beside him. His gun twisted about, but a shattering blow caught him upon the back of the head. His momentum carried him forward. He was aware of the girl just ahead of him. His clawing hands reached out, and cloth caught and tore in his hand. He heard the crash of his automatic remotely, and then another blow drove down against his skull. He did not feel his body strike earth, but he knew he was on the ground. There was a damp coldness against his face, like the coldness of death itself. He fought to rise, to roll and turn. His head moved a little before the last blow drove his face into the earth. His senses exploded in a flash of blue-white pain within his skull!

# CHAPTER 7
# JUDGMENT IN HELL

IT SEEMED to Wentworth that, even in the depths of unconsciousness, he was fighting. When he swam back to a realization of his surroundings, the pain was intolerable. He stirred feebly, and heard Nita cry out above him, heard the harsh tones of Kirkpatrick.

"Well, what are you waiting for?" Kirkpatrick snapped. "Get him on the stretcher!"

Wentworth opened his eyes with a protest. "Not… necessary, Kirk," he whispered. "Nita will take me home… What about McMann… and the others?"

Kirkpatrick did not answer for a moment, and Wentworth focused his eyes more clearly. He saw the black tracery of leaves above him, lighted by shafts of flashlights. Strong hands were under his arms, and he turned his splitting head to look into Ram Singh's grave eyes.

Wentworth got to his feet, reeled and clamped his teeth to shut back the groan of pain. "Well, Kirk?" he gasped. "What about the three?"

"Gone!" Kirkpatrick said. "The killers had a car hidden in the woods. They smashed a gate. Machine-gunned five policemen on guard there. Got clean away."

Wentworth's breath gusted out. He looked curiously down at his right hand, and saw that it grasped a torn fragment of red silk.

"I was close to them," he whispered. "Close enough to catch a

91

handful of silk from Anne's dress. I was hit three times—faster, I think, than one person could strike. How long have I been completely out, Kirk?"

"About an hour," Kirkpatrick said flatly. "Dick, if you won't go to a hospital, you're going straight home. A concussion like that is dangerous! There should be X-rays."

"Yes, yes," Wentworth agreed. "If they're gone, there's nothing can be done. Nothing at all. But if one of those butcher shops—a Schultz shop—is near here, you shouldn't neglect it!"

"We'll take care of it," Kirkpatrick said grimly. "Nita."

"Yes, Stanley," Nita said to Kirkpatrick. "He's going home right now—I'll see to it!"

Wentworth did not protest. He leaned heavily on Ram Singh's shoulder as he was guided toward his big Daimler limousine. He sank back gratefully, let his aching head rest gingerly against the cushions. They passed the police guards before Wentworth spoke.

"An hour," he said slowly. "Too late to save the first victim. But Judge Torture wouldn't spoil his pleasure by tormenting all three at one time. Especially when he thinks he has got clean away."

Nita said, emphatically, "Dick, you're going home!"

Wentworth ignored the interruption. "The dead man in the clock was one of the three thugs at the Frisco Club. He was undoubtedly killed last night... and yet *rigor mortis* was just getting under way. Their previous headquarters have been butcher shops, and there is only one way to delay *rigor mortis* in the dead. Immediate and complete freezing!"

"Refrigeration!" Nita gasped. "The Schultz cold storage plant! I'll get in touch with Kirkpatrick." She reached for the microphone and switch of the two-way radio.

Wentworth rested his hand on her arm. "Search warrants take time," he said, "even if Kirkpatrick could get a judge to issue one. There is no evidence for such a request, and we cannot tell Kirkpatrick how we know about the

NITA VAN SLOAN

93

mutilated thug. I am not supposed to have seen those three criminals at the Frisco Club!"

Nita's face was drawn with concern. "But, Dick! Your poor head!"

Wentworth's face was pale, his lips drawn thinly against his teeth. His voice came out hoarsely, strained. "Ram Singh, go to the Schultz cold storage plant!" His hand reached out, manipulated the ashtray. The glass panels slid up and the windows of the limousine turned opaque. Wentworth touched the button that opened the secret wardrobe of the Spider....

THERE WAS no order in the court of Judge Torture in the usual judicial sense of the term. Noise was almost constant, and it brought forth hissing laughter from the bench where the red-robed figure sat.

The noise was caused by the groans of Judge Torture's victims.

There were eight of these victims tonight, summoned to the midnight session. There had been some slight difficulty in bringing three of them, but they were all here—waiting the judgment of Judge Torture!

At least, seven of them were still waiting. One had already faced that judgment: Phideas McMann.

He was no longer protesting, even in groans. His body had been twisted upon a steel frame so that it no longer seemed a human body. It was a grotesque dollar mark.

Phideas McMann was dead.

Dressed in his crimson silken robes, Judge Torture sat immobile behind the high rostrum of the bench. The white wig and the black cap upon his head were conspicuous, but his face remained in black shadow. The bench was flanked by guards wearing the long antique doublets of an older day, and carrying in their hands metal-pointed tipstaffs. The three men who had conducted the torture of Phideas McMann were stripped to the waist. They stood at attention beside the human dollar mark, waiting orders.

There was no need to guard the seven other victims.

Overhead ran a steel rail, depended from the ceiling. Wheeled pulleys were attached to that rail, pulleys that ended in sharp pointed hooks and were intended to transport heavy sides of beef through the refrigeration plant. From those hooks, hung the victims.

Most of them had been carefully hung so as not to weaken them too much for the ordeal that lay ahead. Morris Bacon's right palm had been pierced. His feet almost touched the floor. Anne Bacon, considerately, dangled by her knotted hair.

Judge Torture was speaking. "This gentleman, McMann," he said in his slow, mocking way, "could have been profitably fined. But an example was required. He will serve... as a warning that Judge Torture must be obeyed!

"The rest of you will not have the opportunity of seeing him exhibited, and that is regrettable... so it is only fair that you should be told. This court insists on fairness!"

Judge Torture laughed grimly.

Morris Bacon lifted his dangling head and looked toward the bench, let his head sag again. He hung off by himself in the shadows. It was apparent that a special fate was reserved for him.

"Our dollar mark will be carried tonight to Wall Street,"

Judge Torture resumed. "He will become the capital frieze of Trinity Church, where all the denizens of Wall Street can see and properly appreciate *the justice of Judge Torture!*"

Judge Torture was silent after that. A man groaned upon his hook, and a woman sobbed.

"Take him away," Judge Torture ordered, and the tormenters wheeled away the body of McMann. From the shadows, Judge Torture's unseen eyes glowed. His laughter sounded.

"Yes, my dear, you have not much longer to wait," he said. "I fancy, my friend Bacon, that Anne is indicated as our next... prisoner at the bar!"

Bacon's head lifted. He cursed lividly. "Kill me and have done with it!" he said fiercely. "Why must you destroy my brother, and my daughter!"

JUDGE TORTURE chuckled, "For discipline, my dear Bacon! And while you are waiting, consider the possibilities of the letter X. By fastening arms and legs securely to the split halves of an upright, and then slowly separating those halves... You get the idea? Yes, I see that you do. Of course, it may be necessary to employ knives or even saws. We have had some remarkable demonstrations of the toughness of human skin, and muscles, and bones. Very stubborn and difficult for your true artist!"

Bacon groaned, but made no answer, and Judge Torture laughed again.

"I shall leave you to your contemplations while we *initial* Anne Bacon! Bailiff, bring the prisoner before the bar!"

One of the bailiffs marched stiffly to where Anne was

suspended, placed lewd hands upon her body. He pushed her along the steel rail. The hook's pulley squeaked. Anne gasped at the fresh pain. There was blood in the roots of her hair. The bailiff swung her about to face the bench.

"You, my dear," purred Judge Torture, "were most obdurate. Out of vanity, you defied my orders!"

Anne's voice was tortured and hoarse. "Oh, no!" she cried. "Oh, please—"

"Oh, please—*your honor,*" Judge Torture suggested gently.

Anne bit her lips. "Oh, please... your honor," she whispered.

"We are inclined to be merciful with you," Judge Torture said equably, "but such vanity must be punished. Now, let me see... something simple, for simplicity is the essence of art!"

The torturers returned. They stood, with folded arms, and their eyes rested on the body of the dangling girl. Their eyes glistened. About them were the shadows of the vast cold storage plant. The room was high ceilinged. The far wall contained a dozen doorways through each of which ran the steel rails with their dangling, hooked pulleys. From high in the darkness descended a steel cable that slanted down to a floor vat, covered now, which was used for scalding porkers. A gleam of light seemed to flicker for an instant in that high darkness, but no one appeared to notice. Judge Torture, still motionless, was intent upon the girl before him.

"I have it now," he said, with satisfaction. "It is simple, merciful—and salutary! For, see you, my dear Anne, nothing is more explicit of vanity than... the first person singular pronoun! Yes, Anne, I shall convert you into a capital *I.*"

A HOARSE cry issued from Anne's lips. Her bound wrists wrenched at their bonds, and she gyrated by her knotted hair, until the hands of the bailiff stopped her. A bead of blood seeped from her hair roots down across her temple.

"Really," Judge Torture said tartly, "one would almost say that you do not appreciate my mercy! I could not have been pleasanter to you! A mere matter of removing all excrescences to make sure that you are completely vertical. We will begin with the arms, severed at the shoulder!"

Anne screamed as she was lifted from the hook by the rough hands of the half-naked butchers. They carried her swiftly to a heavy block of wood, flung her across it, back down.

Judge Torture said, softly, "Just use the cleavers, my man. I wish to be merciful!"

There was laughter then in that hollow vault which Judge Torture used for a courtroom. It was mocking, as the laughter of Judge Torture had been, but it was more menacing, colder... It was flat and metallic.

It was the laughter of the Spider!

Even while it sounded, those butchers with uplifted cleavers, those bailiffs with their deadly tipstaffs, cried out in hoarse fright. They stiffened and stared into the darkness about them. On the bench, Judge Torture did not move at all. But the victims, on their hooks, twisted up affrighted faces that were white with hope... and yet incredulous in their despair.

There was a thin, singing note of metal drawn swiftly over metal... and suddenly, the Spider was upon them!

Gliding down that steel cable which slanted from above, the

Spider dangled by one hand from a pulley hook. His gun was in his fist, and his black robes whipped out wildly behind him.

"Death!" cried the Spider. "Death to Judge Torture!"

But the butcher's cleaver already was striking down at Anne Bacon's outstretched arm. The Spider flung his first shot there. There was the ring of steel and the cleaver flashed from the man's hand, glittered off into the darkness. The man was driven sideways by the impact of the first bullet, and the next caught him beneath the ear.

And still the Spider sailed through the air, ten feet above the floor!

He twisted his deadly gun about… and the space behind the bench was vacant! Judge Torture had vanished!

A cry of thwarted anger burst from the Spider's lips, but his gun was speaking again. The two bailiffs pitched writhing to the floor before the high rostrum where Judge Torture had sat. The other two torturers tried to dash off into the darkness… but the Spider's lead was too swift. They sprawled headlong, kicking out their lives on the floor.

The Spider reached the floor. His feet swept ahead to take up the momentum of his swift dash down the wire. They groped for footing… and failed to find it. The Spider stumbled and fell to the floor. He was slow in rising, and his legs were braced widely apart. His eyes had a feverish glisten.

Anne Bacon lay in a faint across the butcher's block. The other victims… The Spider's eyes swept them, and sick horror smote him. His gun stayed in his hand as he moved toward the men and women who dangled from those fearful hooks. He went feverishly to work to free them. It was frantic work for a man already three quarters out on his feet. There was an agony within his skull that his fall had not improved. His horror at the scene was like physical torment. Finally, the last of the victims was lifted to the floor. Only two stood upon their feet. The others had fainted. Anne Bacon was pushing her body up from the butcher's block on which she lay.

Her eyes went wonderingly to the Spider. "You—you saved my life," she whispered.

WENTWORTH BOUNDED past her, toward the rostrum and stared down at the floor. A trap-door, as he had expected! He set furiously to work upon it. It had been impossible to pursue Judge Torture while these people dangled in torment upon their hooks, and now—now it would be too late! Wentworth cursed hoarsely as he sought the means to manipulate the trapdoor.

Then he straightened, staring down at a pair of fine, insulated wires caught in the crack. The Spider recalled that he had not seen Judge Torture actually *move* in the time he had looked upon him on the rostrum. He recalled, too, that always when he had heard him, Judge Torture had spoken over a microphone to disguise his voice!

Almost certainly, then, Judge Torture had not himself been seated behind the rostrum! Instead, he had been hidden somewhere near, had spoken over a microphone. At the first hint of danger, he had dumped the effigy of himself through the trapdoor in the floor! He had hoped that the Spider would be diverted into following that false trail!

Wentworth crouched behind the rostrum and pulled out his second, fully loaded, automatic. His eyes quested into the darkness. Somewhere there, Judge Torture might still be lurking, awaiting his opportunity to strike! The Spider's lips grinned back from his teeth as he fought the whirling of his brain. Let him strike; the Spider was ready!

The voice that spoke came from behind Wentworth. It was a young voice, hoarse with strain. It said, "Up with your hands, Spider!"

Wentworth's gun pivoted in his hand. He did not need to see in order to shoot accurately. A twist, a squeeze on the trigger, and the man who spoke would be dead! But, strangely, Wentworth did not shoot.

Instead, he turned slowly about—and a gasp tore from his throat.

He was looking into the black, steady eye of a revolver, and into the intent, white face of—Jack Murdock!

## CHAPTER 8
## THE WARNING

A TREMOR of reaction raced through the Spider's tautly strung body. He had keyed himself up with stimulants for this attack, and his strength was leaving him. There was a dull throbbing agony within his head. He was nearly ill at having come so close to killing Jack Murdock!

Wentworth faced Murdock, his disguised face expressionless, as he studied the boy's eyes. But he was remembering that

Murdock had been jailed as a material witness not so many hours before. It was extraordinary that he should have been released so soon unless—unless, as Nita feared, he was a servant of Judge Torture!

Wentworth's eyes studied the boy's face keenly, and involuntarily he shook his head. Unless all his judgment of men was wrong, this boy was honest.

Murdock barked, "I said, *'Up with your hands!'* "

Wentworth shook his head. "I think not, Murdock. You were very close to death a few moments ago. I almost shot before I knew who you were. And you'd better get out of here quickly. The police will have heard a report of the shooting, probably...."

Murdock smiled slightly, "I telephoned them before I came in here. But not to catch you. I don't play the game that way. Spider, I'm warning you! You killed my dad, and I'm gunning for you! The next time our trails cross—I'll shoot on sight!"

Wentworth nodded quietly. "Fair enough," he said.

Murdock swallowed stiffly, "You don't deny that you killed my dad!" he said. "You don't even try to excuse yourself? It—it wasn't an accident, maybe?"

Wentworth shook his head slowly. "It wasn't an accident, Murdock," he said. "I followed your father—and killed him. He had an even break with his gun, but that doesn't enter into it."

"No," Murdock said thickly, "that doesn't enter into it!"

Around the rostrum, Wentworth saw Anne Bacon, in her torn crimson dress, move slowly toward the boy. She said, hesitantly. "Mr. Murdock, the Spider saved my life!"

Wentworth moved a hand impatiently. He could catch the

faint whimper of police sirens beyond the thick walls. "Let me get you out of here, Murdock," he said. "I don't know how you got out of jail...."

"Mr. Wentworth bailed me out!" Murdock said defiantly.

Wentworth's eyes narrowed, but he made no comment.

"I promised Mr. Wentworth I wouldn't hunt you up, Spider," Murdock hurried on, "and I didn't. I saw Mr. Wentworth's car stop near here, and when I followed him to thank him, I heard a gun inside. I called the cops and came on in."

Wentworth nodded briskly. "All right, Murdock, I'm glad to hear you're a man of your word. But if the police find you here...."

Murdock's jaw set stubbornly. "I'll just tell them the truth!" he said stiffly.

Anne Bacon said, gently, "I'll tell them the truth, too, and they can't hold Mr. Murdock for just coming in here!"

Jack Murdock let the gun sag down to his side and turned his head toward the girl. "That's mighty nice of you... Anne," he said.

Anne Bacon smiled up hesitantly at him, and then together they looked back toward the Spider. Jack Murdock cried out hoarsely, sprang toward the rostrum. On its surface there gleamed the mocking red seal of the Spider! On the floor, there were a few red splattered drops as if the Spider had been wounded. But the Spider himself... had vanished!

THE FIRST two radio police to reach the warehouse leaped from their coupé and sprinted toward the main door of the cold storage plant. They forced the door with quick blows and then, seemingly from behind them, they heard the harsh and rasping laughter of the Spider!

The men whirled about, and the laughter came to their ears again. They caught a glimpse of light from a dark doorway!

Instantly, their guns were in their fists and they were racing toward that dark doorway. Out of a window, near the warehouse door, a black shadow slipped. It glided along the base of the wall and merged with the darkness of the street.

Instants later, a long black limousine slipped from the curb and went whirling away while the police still searched the darkness of the tenement across the street from the warehouse.

"It was simple enough," Wentworth explained to Nita as he stripped off the disguise of the Spider. "I simply threw my laughter against the opposite wall, made the hooded beam of my flashlight reflect from the glass panel of a door. They thought I was across the street, and it gave me the few seconds I needed to get clear!"

Nita's eyes were very large in the pale oval of her face. "You're wounded, Dick!" she said quietly. "Your right hand—"

Wentworth glanced down at it casually. "Tore it on the meat hook I used for transportation, I guess," he said. "A smear of collodion and a bit of paint will cover it... I'll be very much surprised if Anne Bacon and Jack Murdock don't presently discover that they love each other... Did you arrange for Murdock to be bailed out?"

Nita shook her head. "No, of course not, Dick."

Wentworth frowned slightly as he leaned back against the cushions and closed his eyes. He was once more Richard Wentworth, and the opaque panels of glass had been lowered into their sockets.

"Murdock is under the impression that I bailed him out," he said slowly. "I don't quite understand this move!"

"Oh, but I do!" Nita cried softly. "Judge Torture!"

Wentworth frowned and did not answer. He could not believe that Murdock was a servitor of Judge Torture... but what other explanation could there be for this strange bail bond?

Ram Singh's voice came back sharply from the driver's seat. "Police car coming toward us, *sahib!*" he said. "It could be the car of Kirkpatrick *sahib!*"

"Signal him to stop!" Wentworth cried swiftly.

The Daimler's headlights flashed brilliantly, died, flashed again. Wentworth punched open the door of the car. "Just follow my lead, Nita," he whispered, and stepped to the street to wave his arms above his head in signal to the car.

The big limousine of the police commissioner heaved to a halt, and Kirkpatrick peered out the window.

"Dick," Kirkpatrick snapped. "I ordered you home! What are you doing here?"

Wentworth was a little uncertain on his feet as he moved toward Kirkpatrick, with Nita behind him. "I thought maybe cool air would help," he said. "I went for a drive on the westside highway... but I had an idea that couldn't wait. Kirk, McMann and the others will undoubtedly be found dead, tortured as these other men have been. Kirk, the police must find those bodies first, and their discovery must be kept secret!"

Kirkpatrick opened the door of his car, motioned Wentworth

and Nita inside. "Why a secret?" he asked as they settled themselves against the cushions.

Wentworth's voice came out vigorously in spite of his weariness. "It's perfectly obvious that Judge Torture plans a campaign of terrorization. We can deprive him of half his power, if we do not allow that terrorization to spread!"

Kirkpatrick knuckled his mustache and did not comment. "Why did you bail out that Murdock boy?" he demanded flatly.

Wentworth said, "What? Bail out Murdock?"

"You mean you didn't do it?" Kirkpatrick's words were sharp. "But the lawyer said he represented you! He put up cash bail!"

Wentworth said, "I didn't do it, Kirk. Who was the lawyer?"

Kirkpatrick checked an oath. "Sulliman was the attorney. I should have been suspicious of him! You wouldn't use him. Confound it, Dick, I don't like the way things are developing! That triple kidnapping when I had a hundred men on the estate! And there have been a dozen other abductions tonight! *We've got to stop Judge Torture!*"

Wentworth shook his head. "You can help to defeat him by keeping these atrocities secret, Kirk, so that they won't serve as warning to others!"

Kirkpatrick's frown grew stubborn and he did not speak again until the car drew to a halt at the Schultz warehouse. "I'm going to have Schultz locked up for twenty-four hours at any rate," he said flatly. He told of the alarm from the warehouse, the mysterious telephone call. "Dick, I want you to go to your home now... Oh, all right! But, confound it, you're not coming inside! You can sit here and cool your heels… and maybe that hot head of yours! You've taken terrific punishment tonight!"

Wentworth was glad of a chance to relax, but his brain kept working at white heat. "We've got to keep these atrocities a secret," he said repeatedly to Nita. "It's the only way we can hamper Judge Torture!"

"Do you think it's Schultz?" Nita asked softly.

Wentworth lifted a shoulder. "Schultz has to be involved in some way. How deeply, I don't know. Otherwise, it would not be possible to use his properties in this way."

He was content not to see again the horrors of the torture room, and it was not until the entire cavalcade of released victims had been taken back to police headquarters that he again confronted Jack Murdock.

Murdock came to him directly, thrust out his hand. "I want to thank you for getting me out on bail, Mr. Wentworth," he said.

Wentworth accepted his hand while repeating his denial of help, and Murdock's hand clamped down with an almost savage violence upon his. Wentworth felt hot pain stab through his hand from the wound in his palm, and suspicion rose as quickly in his brain. Murdock, obviously, had spotted a right-hand wound upon the Spider! Wentworth's face held its slight, deprecating smile and disappointment seemed to darken Murdock's eyes. He stepped back, a muttered apology, and stood beside Anne Bacon.

Wentworth moved past them into Kirkpatrick's private office where he was disposing of two callers before going on with his inquiry. Wentworth entered quietly, but the two men who stood angrily over Kirkpatrick's desk whipped about as if a shot had been fired. Uneasy smiles made their mouths sly.

Kirkpatrick's voice held an impatient rasp, "But I tell you, gentlemen," he was saying, "that so far we have been able to obtain no clue at all to the identity or headquarters of this Judge Torture! Your wisest course, until we can reach him, would be to obey his orders—and trust us to redress matters afterward!"

There was bombast and invective from the two men, but finally they left. Their curses hung in the air behind them. Kirkpatrick sat rigidly behind his desk, his eyes troubled.

"That makes fourteen complaints in addition to all those who have been stricken without asking police help," he said heavily. "There must be many more who have obeyed the orders of Judge Torture without daring to complain."

Wentworth nodded. "There will be many more… if you allow McMann's death to become public," he said. "Especially if the manner of his death is known."

The door swung open and Morris Bacon, his left hand bandaged from the torture of the meat hook, strode in to confront Kirkpatrick.

"I have demanded police protection," he said savagely, "and it hasn't helped at all. Now, I find that you are recommending that citizens submit to this fiendish Judge Torture! My brother has been killed, my daughter and myself tortured! If it had not been for the intervention of still another criminal who calls himself the Spider, we should both be lying dead and horribly mutilated right now! I am through with your shilly-shallying! There is only one cure for this horror… and I shall take it!"

Jack Murdock and Anne had come in at the door and Wentworth stepped to their side, while Bacon continued to shout his indignation at Kirkpatrick.

Wentworth smiled down at Anne. "I'm afraid I tore your dress on McMann's estate," he said gravely. "I caught at you as I fell. It is very lovely silk. Italian, isn't it?"

Anne Bacon smiled frankly. "This silk is my own vanity," she admitted. "I liked the color so well that I bought up all that was produced. It was a limited quantity." She grew a little pale. "Judge Torture accused me of—of vanity!"

Murdock said, grudgingly, "I can't get my mind straight on this Spider. He killed my dad, but he saved Anne—I mean, Miss Bacon. Those guys he killed there deserved to die." His smile was hesitant. "The Commissioner gave me hell for letting the Spider get away, but a guy has to give a man warning. Don't you think so, Mr. Wentworth?"

Wentworth had no chance to answer. Bacon bounced indignantly to the door. "Come, Anne," he snapped. "And you, too, young man, if you wish. I know how to defeat this Judge Torture! Since the police have failed us, I shall arouse the populace against him!"

He went out, slamming the door, and Murdock and Anne went with him. Kirkpatrick still sat rigidly behind his desk. "Dick," he said. "Against my better judgment, I requested Bacon to tell nothing of what had happened before Judge Torture. I shall keep secret what happened to McMann. I believe you are right, and that the only way we can impede this man is by denying him the publicity he needs for terrorization!"

PERHAPS, JUDGE TORTURE anticipated some such move by the police. Or perhaps he was goaded by sheer impotent rage over the Spider's intervention. At any rate, he struck swiftly, within the next twenty-four hours, to gain the publicity the Spider sought to suppress.

In the before-theatre hour, Broadway is always crowded with window-shoppers. The most popular window is that of the rotisserie. That window is festooned with delicately browned roasts of beef and pork and ham. A chef in a high white hat stands over a block and slices the luscious meats. Behind him, there is a vertical grated bank of glowing charcoal and spits, set into its rack, turn freshly cooking meats in the heat.

It was strange then that, just when this crowd was at its peak, the white-capped chef of one rotisserie leaned forward and carefully drew down a shade which covered the entire window!

His act evoked a considerable curiosity. Men tried to peer around the edges of the shade. But the obscurity did not endure long; perhaps two minutes. Then the shade went up again.

At first, a man laughed at what he saw. A woman's voice lifted in indignation. And then, an incredulous silence fell. The man who had laughed turned pallid. A greenish white showed about his mouth. He turned abruptly away from the window, fighting with both arms to gain his way to freedom. His breath was strangled in his throat. The woman screamed.

Her cry rose to incredible shrillness. Its sound went on and on, longer than it seemed possible for breath to last. It quit on a gasping inhalation, and then the scream began again.

It was still sounding, when the crowd broke into a milling

panic. A woman fainted to the sidewalk. A man beat at the glass window with his closed fists. Another ran shouting along the pavement.

"Hey, police!" he yelled. "Police! There's a murder!"

In a space of seconds there was no one at all before the window, though traffic was jamming in the street and men and women craned their necks from cars. The white-capped chef had disappeared now. The savory meats were gone from the carving blocks. But one laden spit still revolved before the vertical bank of the charcoal fire. What the spit held... was no ordinary roast. It was a girl's naked body. Her flesh was already beginning to brown, delicately.

THERE WAS another window before which a crowd invariably gathered at this hour of the night. It was further down town—the huge window behind which roared the presses of one of the city's biggest newspapers. The spinning cylinders, the intricate weaving of the virgin paper, and its emergence in thick-packed streams of printed news sheets, offered ceaseless attraction.

It was about a half hour after the affair in the rotisserie window that the lights of the press room darkened for a space of a moment, then flared again.

The presses began to rumble when the lights lifted. A man's hoarse screaming burst from inside. It was formless, without words... the frantic sounds that a trapped animal might make.

The crowd outside the window saw him a moment later. There was a rope around his neck. His arms and feet were bound...

and the rope about his neck led between two of the great steel cylinders of the press!

One of the crowd beat frantically on the window. The glass crashed and he shouted above the roar of the presses. But the man who should have stopped the mighty machine lay motionless beside the switch. The presses continued to roll.

The screams mounted to a frenzy of pain and terror... and were crushed out.

MOVEMENT CALLED the attention of people to Judge Torture's third victim. Movement, and darkness, where there should have been light.

It was not terribly high above the level of the street. The electric signs that dance along Times Square are placed where men can see them readily. That is also why they are brightly illuminated; why the colors dance and cavort in intricate patterns—and why this particular spot of darkness was seen.

It was a large sign, advertising a motion picture. It was a solid bank of glowing white light that wavered and blacked out to shine again. The letters of the words blazed in contrasting red, winking dark when the brilliant white background shone, quivering like fire when the background was dark.

Against that white background, two more dark letters presently made themselves visible. They were grotesque characters, but there was no mistaking that they were the initials *J. T.*

It was some time before the hysterical crowd realized how those letters were formed. They only knew that human bodies had been twisted, alive, into shapes which human bodies could not assume... and continue to live.

Yet one of those men so twisted still screamed and jerked at the stumps which were all that was left of his arms....

THE FOURTH publicity gag of Judge Torture occurred on the stage at the Metropolitan. The overture died into the strains of the opening chorus, and the rich curtain lifted to the faint welcoming applause of the audience.

Then the applause ceased, and the orchestra crashed into discordant silence. Afterward, of course, there were screams and the audience raced in wild panic toward the already choked exits.

But back on the stage, the diva of the show did not move. That is, she did not move with any symptom of life. She swayed gently back and forth, she gyrated slowly to left, and to right, at the end of her rope.

The rope had been tied to her ribs... after the flesh was removed.

RICHARD WENTWORTH was with Kirkpatrick at headquarters when the first hysterical report of the rotisserie horror came over the phone. He went with Kirkpatrick into the restaurant, where the shade had once more been drawn on the pitiful flesh upon the spit.

It was quite plain how the thing had been managed. There was a screen of artificial green between the spit and the restaurant proper, and a trapdoor that led into the basement. They found the chef with his white cap jammed down over his brows by a blow, lying dead upon the basement floor.

Kirkpatrick was throwing sharp questions at his men, and at the owners of the restaurant, but Wentworth was examining the body of the dead chef. His face was drawn thin by the tension of his mouth. Judge Torture had successfully circumvented their ban on publicity. Nothing on earth could prevent the story of these atrocities—and their perpetrator—from being shrieked hysterically via newspaper headline and radio throughout the city.

Suddenly, Wentworth's eyes narrowed, and there was a pinched whiteness about his nostrils. It was true that the deeds themselves could not be kept quiet… but the author? Judge Torture had done nothing here to reveal his true identity! Perhaps he had been confident that the truth would be blazoned forth; perhaps, he counted on revealing his authorship at a later date.

Wentworth's lips drew into a bitter smile as he bent ever lower over the murdered chef. His right hand made a furtive trip to his vest pocket before he pushed aside the white cap. For a long moment, it hesitated over the man's forehead.

Then he straightened with a jerk.

"Kirk!" he cried. "For God's sake. Kirk!"

Commissioner Kirkpatrick whipped about and saw Wentworth standing rigidly, pointing down at the dead man.

"I thought," Wentworth stammered, "that this must be the work of Judge Torture, but another criminal has claimed responsibility. Look!"

Kirkpatrick took two long strides and glared down at the dead man, at the forehead where Wentworth pointed.

Kirkpatrick's oath was strangled, incredulous. "The seal!" he whispered. *"The seal of the Spider!"*

"Yes," Wentworth whispered, too. "The Spider must have

gone mad! This seal proves that… the Spider murdered that poor girl up there!"

Kirkpatrick stared at Wentworth and for once no words came to his lips. He shook his head, looked at the seal and back to Wentworth. It was Wentworth who spoke.

"If the Spider wants credit for this crime," he said slowly. "Surely, he should be allowed to claim it! At least, it will minimize the publicity which Judge Torture might receive!"

Kirkpatrick shook his head, turned away… but a police officer had already shouted incredulously the fact that gleamed, scarlet and menacing, from the forehead of the dead man. Up above, other men caught up the cry. Moments later, that fact was on the radio, blistering the headlines of the newspapers.

Within moments, too, Inspector Littlejohn dropped into the basement, turned the hot blue flames of his eyes upon the dead man, and then on Wentworth.

"When I looked at the dead man, ten minutes ago," he said, "that seal was not on his forehead! It's damned curious that the seal appears only after Wentworth has arrived!"

Wentworth shook his head, and his smile was weary. "You'll have to do better than that, Little John," he said. "I myself was the first to disturb the chef's cap. It was plain that it was in exactly the same position it occupied when driven down over his forehead by the murderer's blow. No, Littlejohn, that trap won't work. But, Kirk, if it disturbs your organization, perhaps I would better withdraw?"

Kirkpatrick nodded curtly. "You can't help here," he said. "As a matter of fact. I think it would be preferable for you to withdraw from the case entirely. There has been too much happening—when you are around!"

Wentworth flushed, clicked his heels in a formal bow. "Just as you wish, Kirkpatrick," he said coldly.

He marched from the basement. Littlejohn whirled to a subordinate. "Have that man followed!" he snapped.

KIRKPATRICK DID not countermand the order, though pain tightened his eyes. "Littlejohn," he said quietly, "you had not looked at the dead man's forehead?"

Littlejohn said stiffly, "No, sir! I was trying to trap him! Damn it, Commissioner, every time the Spider has appeared in this case, Wentworth has shown up just afterward! And this last! I am willing to swear that Wentworth put that seal on the dead man! He was beside the body; he found the seal!"

Kirkpatrick shook his head slowly, "It is not proof, Littlejohn. Send word to set a guard over the other atrocities that have been reported. Rather, set traps! Have the men keep watch and see whether... Wentworth attempts to imprint seals!"

Littlejohn sprang toward the steps... and it was a half hour before he came back. Rage was in his stride, and his eyes sparkled with fury.

"Too late!" he snapped. "The lights went out at one place, before I could get there. At another, somebody opened fire on the cops and drew them away—and in each case, the Spider seal was on the forehead of the victim!"

"But the man on Wentworth's trail?" Kirkpatrick snapped.

Littlejohn shook his head, smiling thinly. "I should have picked my man... or put a full squad on the job!" he said. "He

116

saw Wentworth buy a ticket to a show, and expected him to stay there! As a matter of fact, when we went into the theatre, Wentworth *was* there! But that proves nothing."

Kirkpatrick shook his head dourly, and the pain did not leave his eyes. "No, Inspector, it proves nothing either way!"

It was a painful task that lay before Kirkpatrick, but the facts could not be contradicted in newspapers that already were on the street. The Spider was blamed for the crimes which Kirkpatrick knew in his heart Judge Torture had committed. He would have known that even if those grotesque human initials—J.T.—had not dangled against the face of the electric sign... The papers brought the news also of Morris Bacon's threat to take the case to the people. He was indulging in rabble rousing, talking on street corners and over the radio, and now he had a target for his threats... *the Spider!*

"It is true the Spider saved me, or appeared to save me from a mountebank called Judge Torture," Bacon said, "but I am convinced that was a show put on to convince me and the other victims of the Spider's innocence. It is conspicuous that, with the exception of McMann, none of us was injured enough to be unable to testify to the good works of the Spider!"

It was as a climax to this night of horror that Kirkpatrick found on his desk... a summons from Judge Torture!

"**YOU ARE** hereby summoned, with the following twelve heads of police departments," he read, "to appear before the court of judgment tomorrow midnight... under *pain* of the displeasure of Judge Torture!"

Kirkpatrick swore violently and, in a brace of minutes, had

117

the high officials of the police department before him. But there was no clue as to how the summons had been delivered; or who had brought it there.

Slowly, and with foreboding, Kirkpatrick read out the rest of the summons to the twelve men who were called with him.

"... and if you shall fail to obey this summons," read Kirkpatrick, "there shall be five citizens of New York tortured to slow death for each hour's delay of each man in reporting to said court of judgment."

Kirkpatrick lifted his head and the faces of his twelve subordinates matched his for sternness and determination.

"Gentlemen," Kirkpatrick said slowly, "this matter will be kept a secret in so far as humanly possible. I cannot dictate to the rest of you, if I would, but for me there can be only one choice. I shall obey the summons of Judge Torture—and destroy him!"

The voices of the twelve police officials were a single rumble of sound... and it was assent!

"We'll all go, sir." It was Inspector Littlejohn who spoke. "If the twelve of us can't take this Judge Torture... then we'll deserve what we get!"

Kirkpatrick's face broke into a slow smile. "Excellently put. Inspector," he said. "Gentlemen, I accept your... volunteering. There is no need to speak of rewards. But if we are successful, none of you shall lose by this!"

Inspector Littlejohn's eyes were hot. "Where do we go?"

Kirkpatrick shook his head, "The instructions read that, precisely at midnight, in three cars, we are to drive through Central Park, entering at the southern end. Gentlemen, I do not want you to go into this with your eyes closed. You all know how horribly people have been tortured. There is a chance that… all of us will fail, that all the precautions I can take in the way of police lookouts will fail. If that happens…."

Littlejohn said crisply, "Then we get twisted into various initials… or get a little red seal on our foreheads! But we won't fail! We'll get Judge Torture… and we'll get the Spider at the same time!"

Kirkpatrick's lips twisted. For a moment he stood rigidly, and then he bowed his head in assent.

"Tomorrow night," he said slowly, "will see the end of Judge Torture and the Spider—or the end of us!"

## CHAPTER 9
## REIGN OF TORTURE

NOT MANY blocks away, the Spider climbed wearily into his car and leaned back against the cushions through long minutes before he could stir himself to strip off his habiliments of terror.

"Home," he ordered Ram Singh quietly.

It was possible the blow might fall there. He had given Judge Torture every chance to strike at the Spider tonight after infuriating him by claiming the tortured dead strewn about the city. He had shown himself tauntingly in criminal dives; he had personally invaded every Schultz store and subsidiary. He had even evaded the police on guard there to slip into Schultz's home… but the man himself seemed to have vanished!

119

There had been brushes with the criminals. The Spider had struck down four who had ignored his orders to leave town, and had turned upon him. Twice, Wentworth had narrowly escaped from the guns of the underworld. But about Judge Torture, to whom he had thus offered himself as prisoner, he had learned nothing at all!

So perhaps now, Judge Torture would strike at him at his home. Even his tireless body must rest sometimes… Wentworth thought flashingly of Kirkpatrick, and there was a brief softening of the harsh line of his lips. Never before had he challenged Kirkpatrick so openly as by that imprintation of the Spider's seal; there had been bitter disappointment in Kirkpatrick's eyes.

But never before had the Spider battled such an enemy as Judge Torture!

And the use of the seal had accomplished much. The newspapers and the radio were full of the daring of the Spider, and the horror of his "crimes." The press spoke slightingly of a man named Judge Torture who was trying to capitalize on the Spider's kills—and how his multiple summonses had been generally ignored! There was every reason to believe that Judge Torture would strike at once to eliminate the Spider. Yet he had not done it!

Wentworth tried to find some explanation in his fertile brain for the silence of Judge Torture, under this stern provocation. He knew that it must be a false silence. Somewhere Judge Torture was preparing to strike—but where?

The silence of Judge Torture continued throughout the day. There were no fresh atrocities. If men had disappeared, this fact had not yet been discovered. And Wentworth's apprehension grew. Twice he tried to reach Kirkpatrick by telephone, and his friend had refused to speak to him.

Fiercely, Wentworth conned the newspapers columns and the news broadcasts for some clue to Judge Torture's next blow. There were multiple stories of the police quest for the Spider. That much, at least, Kirkpatrick had heeded the sacrifice Wentworth had made. Morrie Bacon was organizing a torch-light procession to end with a midnight mass meeting in City Hall Square. They would carry banners demanding, *"Death to the Spider!"*

Bacon fulminated for a column on the laxity of the police who, for years, had allowed this super-criminal to work unhindered in the city.

"It is true," Bacon was quoted, "that for a time the Spider masqueraded as a humanitarian, but now at last he flies his true colors! He had tortured helpless men and women to death!"

THERE WAS also an interview with Jack Murdock, and it was clear that his simple honesty had caught the admiration of the newspaper men. Bacon had engineered that, and Anne had told her story. Wentworth frowned over these stories, though they were precisely what he had sought when he imprinted his seals on the victims of Judge Torture.

Was it possible that Judge Torture... feared the Spider too much to strike? Was he waiting for the police to perform his work of vengeance for him?

It was not long before midnight when Wentworth once more fared forth, and this time he went alone in one of the shabby, but powerful, coupés which he kept hidden about the city. He had determined upon a bold maneuver.

The Spider would call on Kirkpatrick! If he could win police cooperation, he thought he had a plan which would capture Judge Torture! The Spider would offer himself as bait, put himself in police hands—if Kirkpatrick would agree to publicize his transportation or imprisonment in such a way that Judge Torture would consider it feasible to kidnap him!

A dozen blocks from police headquarters, Wentworth checked the coupé and blacked out its window, prepared to transform himself once more into the Spider. There was a light shower falling and it whispered softly on the roof. Under the cowling, the radio brought him the voice of a newscaster who shielded himself in mystery and purported to give secret information on the news. He called his program, "The Listening Post."

His muted, falsely hushed voice was coming over the air now. He broke in on his words with, "*Flash!* We have just learned that Police Commissioner Kirkpatrick and twelve of his leading officials left headquarters five minutes ago on a mysterious errand. Even the rest of the police do not know where he has gone, but your Listening Post knows. They have received orders from the mysterious criminal known as Judge Torture... *orders which they dare not disobey!* Yes, ladies and gentlemen, your police commissioner tonight is taking orders from a murderer!"

Wentworth swore harshly and cut short his preparations to transform himself into the Spider. If the announcer spoke the truth, and Kirkpatrick was heading this way... Wentworth whipped the coupé forward, shot across to Lafayette Street. Almost certainly, Kirkpatrick would be summoned northward in Manhattan, and Wentworth intended to intercept him! If Kirkpatrick was indeed accepting orders from Judge Torture, then the Spider was going to be on hand!

He whirled into Lafayette Street and within a few moments, spotted three limousines which bored steadily northward. He whipped his coupé into motion.

Those cars bore police license plates, but the men who drove them did not wear uniform. Wentworth made a hurried count of the men in the cars… thirteen, as the announcer had said. But where was Kirkpatrick? Wentworth could visualize Kirkpatrick accepting orders from Judge Torture all right, but only to trap the criminal. Was he depending on the men who accompanied him, or was he planning an ambush at whatever point his summons bade him to come?

Wentworth's lips shut grimly. If he were to help Kirkpatrick, he must know his plans! He stepped on the gas and rapidly overtook the limousines. The brief shower had stopped now, and the water purred beneath the tires. The street surface picked up the gleam of lights, streaked the windows of the limousines. He could not see clearly through them. But that leading car was Kirkpatrick's.

IT CHECKED at a red traffic signal as a stream of cars slanted across town, and Wentworth ran his coupé alongside. He sprang to the ground, ripped open the door of the limousine… and looked into the blank frightened faces of four men whom he had never seen before!

123

"What are you doing in a police car?" Wentworth snapped at them.

Even as he spoke, Wentworth realized a curious thing. The man nearest him on the rear seat wore Kirkpatrick's hat and coat, complete even to the gardenia upon the lapel! And the other men… Wentworth's eyes swept over them. If he had seen any one of them on the street, he would have taken him for a police official. The man beside the driver wore his hat down over his eyes in precisely the way of Inspector Littlejohn!

The man in Kirkpatrick's coat made a fumbling gesture toward his pocket as if reaching for a gun, and Wentworth's fist struck numbingly upon his wrist.

"None of that!" he snapped. "Come on, speak up! Where is Kirkpatrick?"

But even as he asked that question, his mind was analyzing the situation. If Kirkpatrick had intended this car as a decoy, he would have used police officers… not these timid and frightened men. Moreover, Kirkpatrick would be on the scene already, to find the explanation for an unordered halt!

The man nearest him found speech then. He moistened the lips, swallowed noisily. "Please don't interfere, officer," he said hoarsely. "Please!"

Wentworth flung a swift glance at the other two cars. They had halted just behind this one, bumper-to-bumper. Obviously, they were obeying orders to follow, not acting independently. Wentworth's blue-gray eyes bored into those of the false Kirkpatrick.

"So you obey—*Judge Torture!*" he said softly.

The man's shrinking terror was answer enough, and Wentworth sprang into the car. Guns were instantly in his fists.

"You," he said to the false Kirkpatrick. "Get in my car and drive right beside this one. A single false move, and I'll blast the life out of you! Understand?"

The man moved tremblingly to the street.

"My guns are closer than the threat of Judge Torture!" Wentworth warned.

The man climbed in behind the wheel of the coupé, and Wentworth turned his attention to the driver of the limousine.

"Back to police headquarters!" he snapped.

The man did not hesitate with the cold steel of a gun muzzle boring under his ear. He whipped the car about, and the coupé ran beside it, the other two limousines followed. Wentworth swore softly under his breath. If these men were obeying Judge Torture's orders, it followed that Kirkpatrick and the rest—*were in Judge Torture's power!*

THERE COULD be no other explanation for the fact that they wore the coats and hats of the summoned police officials, and were riding in police cars. Apparently, Kirkpatrick had set some trap at the rendezvous with Judge Torture—and Judge Torture was aware of that fact! He had struck first, seizing Kirkpatrick and the others *before they left headquarters!*

"Faster, damn it!" Wentworth snapped at the driver. "Use that siren!"

Minutes later, the limousines cut to the curb in front of police headquarters and Wentworth leaped to the curb, guns in hand.

"All of you!" he commanded. "Out on the sidewalk! March right into headquarters!"

As he shouted, he heard the door of the headquarters batted open, and the hard clatter of feet beat down the steps between the green lights.

"Put up those guns, Mr. Wentworth!" commanded the voice of Sergeant Reams. "What in hell do you mean, interfering with the commissioner?"

Wentworth twisted his head about, as the doors of the limousines opened. "Look again, Sergeant Reams!" he said. "These men are not the commissioner and the other officials! They are dummies! Get men out here to take charge of them! And follow me to Kirkpatrick's office!"

Wentworth sprang past Sergeant Reams without waiting for more words. He had a brief impression of incredulity on Sergeant Reams' broad, strong face… and a hint of fright, too. But Wentworth waited for no more. He was already plunging through the doors, hammering up the broad steps toward the second floor. Sergeant Reams' voice rang out harshly behind him, calling for men.

Wentworth raced on, pounded into Kirkpatrick's office. It was empty, as Wentworth had known it must be. Against one wall lay the crumpled body of Deputy Commissioner Collins. Burned through his head was the horrible scar that the tipstaff of Judge Torture created!

Wentworth whirled from the room and met Sergeant Reams, who came up at a hard run. "In God's name, Mr. Wentworth," he gasped. "What's happened here?"

Wentworth said shortly, "Judge Torture has kidnapped the commissioner and eleven officials. Collins is dead in there. He must have brought in this phony delegation, marched the commissioner and the other prisoners out in their clothes... left these men here to take their places!"

Sergeant Reams swore and his voice broke. "There was a delegation. The commissioner sent them out by the side door. They walked down the side street to the east. I remember thinking they must be parked there, and wondering why they didn't park out front!"

WENTWORTH DID not wait for the end of his speech. He was darting toward the side exit of headquarters, running along the shower-dampened street. Sergeant Reams ran at his shoulder, still swearing monotously.

"You mean Judge Torture carried them off to kill them?" he panted. "But why in hell didn't the commissioner start shooting, or something?"

"Judge Torture has a weapon," Wentworth said shortly. "If it is pointed at a man, that man is drawn forward like a magnet. That weapon also can kill... It killed Collins."

He rounded the corner, and his eyes swept swiftly over the empty street. No cars parked here at all. There were some bare, dry spots on the pavement where cars had been parked during the rain.

"It was raining when the delegation left?" Wentworth demanded.

"Yes, sir," Sergeant Reams said, "that was why I wondered about them parking here. But it stopped in just a minute."

Wentworth pointed at the bare, dry spots in the street. There were two of them. One had been a car of short wheel base, the other a truck. The broad, double-mark of its rear wheels was there, and the dry spot was very large.

"They were carried off in the truck," Wentworth said quietly. "A small car could not carry off twelve men and their captors."

Sergeant Reams whipped about, "I'll find out who saw this truck here!" he snapped. "We might be lucky!"

Wentworth stooped to the street and picked up a lump of dust from the truck's tracks. Apparently, it had fallen out from between the treads. Wentworth crushed it on his palm. Sergeant Reams checked to stare at him.

"Find something?" he asked harshly.

Wentworth nodded, "I believe I have," he said quietly. "A quantity of vegetable fibers, and—" He lifted the dust to his lips, touched it with his tongue. "—and wheat dust! Sergeant Reams, pace off the length of this truck! Then call out the reserves... and we'll save Commissioner Kirkpatrick!" His lips twisted in pain, and his voice was low and fierce. "We'll save Kirkpatrick—*or avenge his death!*"

INSIDE THE heavy truck, where wheat dust hung suspended in the air like fog, it was close and hot. Kirkpatrick and the eleven officials stood speechless, motionless, save that their bodies swayed to the lurch of the closed lorry.

Their captor was one man and he sat stonily at the end of the truck with a slim wand in his hand, a wand tipped with metal. Now and again, a sly grin upon his mouth, he pointed the wand toward one or another of the men. When he did that, the man strained against his chains and writhed; his head wrenched backward in horrible pain… and the nauseous odor of burning human flesh cloyed the air.

It was thus that Kirkpatrick and his eleven aides made the journey to the Court of Torture. Kirkpatrick's brain was numbed by the intermittent torture of the tipstaff, and by the shock of the thing that had happened. He could have said that it was impossible for any man to do what Judge Torture had achieved in kidnapping twelve officials from the very headquarters of the police… and yet it had been damnably simple to achieve.

The tipstaffs had compelled obedience after poor Collins had been killed; the change of clothing with the men of the delegation and the walk to the truck had been uneventful… and now they were on their way to death through what torments Judge Torture could devise before killing them.

When finally the doors at the rear of the truck swung open, there was only a pitch blackness around them. Then blazing, battering light slammed in through the open doors and blotted out all vision. One by one, the men were freed of their chains, and led, under the compelling power of the tipstaff, through the punishment of that light into darkness beyond. Kirkpatrick was left until last of all and vainly he struggled to discover some clue to his whereabouts. It was useless, and suddenly he realized that even if he discovered the location of this hideout, it would do no good. He was doomed; the men with him were doomed. Judge Torture was supreme!

In that moment of despair, Kirkpatrick thought of one hope… and that was the Spider!

How many times had he been in the midst of death, only to be snatched to safety by that lone wolf of justice who remained outside the law! But this time, even that thin possibility was too remote.

Transiently, Kirkpatrick was conscious of the freshness of the air, a moistness as if a body of water were near; his straining ears caught the *distant*, mournful hoot of a tugboat. Then, once more, the sweet dustiness of wheat-scented air closed about him.

The man who led him forward brushed aside a curtain and, abruptly, Kirkpatrick was in the court of Judge Torture!

He stared about him incredulously. Here were all the trappings of a courtroom; the high rostrum of the judge, the tables for counsel… even the jury box! And in that jury box, their hands chained to rails before them, were the eleven officials who were his fellow prisoners!

But Kirkpatrick was not taken to the empty twelfth seat. Instead, he was kept standing, waiting… before the bar! Kirkpatrick realized only dimly what was in store for him, but one fact was plain enough! His own officials would be required to sit in judgment upon him!

The overhead lights blinked out for perhaps half a second. When they flared on again, Kirkpatrick found himself blinking at the figure behind the rostrum—Judge Torture! The face was shadowed, but the masquerade of the court was carried out in detail: crimson robe, and white wig. And the black cap of sentence perched upon the desk!

The tipstaff bearer banged a gavel and began a formal, practiced chant. "Oyez, oyez, the Court of the Damned, in and for the County of New York, is here and now in session convened. All who may have just cause...."

THE MOCKERY ran on and Kirkpatrick knew a saving anger. His face hardened and his shoulders threw off their dropping despair. That this mad torturer dared to make mockery of human justice!

"Stop this mummery!" Kirkpatrick thundered.

The gavel banged again and Judge Torture spoke calmly from the bench.

"Prisoner before the bar," he said softly, "you are charged with failure to obey the orders of this court. How do you plead?"

Kirkpatrick laughed shortly. His eyes flicked about the room. There were a half-dozen of the bailiffs, each armed with his metal-tipped staff. They stood, evenly spaced, about the curtained walls. Kirkpatrick was chained helplessly to the railing of the dock in which he stood, as his men were secured in the jury box.

Judge Torture did not laugh. His soft voice ran on. "Since you stand mute," he said, "I shall plead you guilty, prisoner before the bar. We have our own methods of procedure here. Sentence is executed before the court... and the jury itself pronounces the full sentence.

"I shall now instruct the jury."

Kirkpatrick's voice was edged with agony. "I do appreciate your pleading me guilty, you crook. I shall have a similar pleasure when you are arraigned!"

Judge Torture ignored him. He was addressing the jury prisoners. "Gentlemen, I will explain the functioning of this court. In order to assure strict justice, we allow the jury itself to pronounce sentence. There is this proviso. If the punishment meted out to the prisoner is not satisfactory to the court, then the court will execute judgment on the juror! Now then…"Judge Torture's voice held a hint of sly amusement. "You have heard the prisoner plead guilty to disobedience of this court's orders. I will instruct you as to possible punishment!"

A buzzer whirred faintly, and beside the judge's bench, the curtains parted. Three men came into the room. Three men naked to the waist, and clad below that in scarlet tights… three men whose faces were hidden by black hoods! And before them, they trundled a low platform set on wheels. It carried a number of articles. There was a brazier in which several irons had been set. They were white hot. There was a rack from which dangled thumb screws for crushing the fingers, and gyves for crushing the legs. There were also various steel tools with pointed tongs, saw-edged cups and forceps whose purpose was not immediately apparent, but which plainly were intended for various mutilations of the human body.

The most prominent item on the platform was a steel cradle large enough for a man, set upon rockers. The inside was studded with spikes.

"My executioners," purred Judge Torture.

The men wheeled the torture truck to a halt before the bench and retired briefly behind the curtain. When they returned, they wheeled a frame of steel. It formed the letter S.

JUDGE TORTURE laughed softly. "I have a weakness for this particular letter," he said. "To create it, with the human body,

132

without immediately killing the prisoner, calls for the utmost skill. One is compelled to sever certain muscles skillfully; the bones must be broken in just the right places. This is particularly true of the spine, for there the slightest miscalculation will result in immediate death. Which, do you see, would deprive the performance of all artistry!

"However, do not worry unduly, my executioners are very skillful. They have had... *practice!*"

Kirkpatrick felt horror crawling coldly through his vitals, but his brain refused to accept the things he heard and saw. Such things could not be done to human beings! They could not be done... and yet Kirkpatrick had seen the horror that could be wrought upon these steel frames by Judge Torture! Kirkpatrick tried to speak, and his throat was dry. He burst out with a furious oath.

"You are not a man!" he cried hoarsely. "You are a monster!"

Judge Torture laughed. He spoke to the jury. "Juror Number One," he said slowly. "You have before you the various punishments which may, under the law, be applied to the prisoner. What is your sentence?"

Kirkpatrick turned slowly to look toward the jury box. It was Inspector Carstairs whom Judge Torture addressed, and Carstairs' jaw was hard set so that muscles stood out lumpily beneath the flesh.

Inspector Carstairs said, clearly, "Go to hell!"

For a space of seconds, there was deathly silence in the court, and then Judge Torture chuckled. "Very childish, Juror Number One," he said, "and no imagination. Also, your sentence is hardly adequate. Our torments are far superior to those devised in hell as man defines it. Therefore, you shall yourself… go to hell—in my own version!"

The executioners waited beside their torture platform, arms folded on powerfully muscled chests. Judge Torture spoke carelessly. "Bring in the griddle," he ordered.

Without a word, the three men filed back through the curtains, and brought out a third platform. It contained only one article—a large sheet of steel under which a white-hot fire blazed. The sheet was smoking. In spots, it glowed cherry red.

The three executioners rolled the griddle to a halt, then they marched toward Inspector Carstairs!

Kirkpatrick raved curses at the imperturbable figure in scarlet, with his wig-shadowed face. Carstairs thrust to his feet and began to fight furiously against the chains that bound him. All the men were on their feet, swearing, cursing, trying to wrench free. But the bar to which they were bound was steel. It held. And the tipstaffs began to focus their wands on the screaming men.

Within a space of seconds, the men were reduced to cowering, whimpering creatures of despair. Their muscles swelled under the torment of the wands. They slumped in their chairs. Even Carstairs seemed stricken to apathy. The three executioners gripped him by the arms, stripped off his clothing with keen knives.

They carried him toward the griddle.

Even when be reached the platform, Carstairs did not resist. He stepped up on the wooden dais. Kirkpatrick wrenched at his chains, felt them bite into his wrists. He tugged futilely at the steel bar of the dock in which he stood.

"Carstairs!" he shouted. "Carstairs, fight! Fight them, man!"

But Carstairs made no resistance... until one of the executioners released his grip to seize a rope. Then Carstairs struck! HE WHEELED upon the edge of the platform, and his fear-mad strength hurled one of the executioners against the griddle. The man's scream lifted in pure agony, and Carstairs leaped upon the second masked torturer. His hand seized the knife from the man's belt, jerked it high... and in that posture, he froze!

The six tipstaffs were focused upon him. They stiffened him rigidly as a statue there beside the torture platform. The executioner whom he had hurled against the griddle slipped to the floor and lay there, moaning. Judge Torture had not spoken.

Carstairs stood rigidly beside the platform, the knife lifted in menace above his head. Muscles bulged under his skin. They writhed like snakes. Before him, the executioner stepped back a slow pace out of the range of the tipstaffs and folded his arms, waiting... waiting while the tipstaffs rendered his prisoner helpless!

Carstairs swore hoarsely. His chest heaved with the effort of breathing. His knees were going lax. With a final, violent wrench, he brought down his knife arm. It had no strength in it.

Carstairs turned his pleading eyes to the face of Kirkpatrick and something like a wan smile touched Carstairs' lips. He plunged, face foremost, to the floor!

Instantly, the executioner leaped toward him. The burned man picked himself up, staggering, from the platform beside

135

the griddle and moved forward to help. Across his back, a great raw burn marked where his flash had touched the iron. He set his hands upon Carstairs and they heaved him up.

A sob knotted in Kirkpatrick's throat. Carstairs had played his last card, and played it well. When he had fallen, it was upon the point of the knife… and he was free of Judge Torture!

That faint smile was still on Carstairs' lips!

Judge Torture's voice rasped harshly. "Put him down, fools!" he snapped. "There is no pleasure in torturing a dead man! Take the next man, and be more careful this time! It might be expedient to break his arms and legs first… break each one twice!

"Well, fools! What are you waiting for?"

The executioners trembled under the lash of Judge Torture's voice. One of them ran, staggering, toward the curtains and brushed them aside. It was the man who had been burned. The other two turned toward the jury box to select another victim.

Kirkpatrick lifted his white face toward the unseeable skies. There was no hope in him, and no longer any strength. There was only great despair. Nothing could save them. Not even the Spider, should he in some incredible way find the court of Judge Torture. Those tipstaffs would immobilize him instantaneously. And Judge Torture would pronounce a new sentence!

It was the rasp of Judge Torture's voice which cut into his thoughts. "You delay a long time, my torturer!" he whispered.

Kirkpatrick pulled his despairing eyes down, and saw the burned torturer finally stagger out from behind those curtains. He carried a heavy sledge hammer. He hurried past in front of the bench, but he moved in such a way that his back was not toward the bench, but toward Kirkpatrick.

Kirkpatrick's eyes widened incredulously. Somehow, in those brief moments, the man had treated his back so that it no longer showed that angry raw weal where red-hot iron had touched it! But he had not dared to reveal that fact to the figure in crimson upon the bench!

"Break his arms first," Judge Torture ordered.

THE TWO torturers dragged the second victim's forearms across the iron bar to which he was chained. It was Deputy Commissioner Martin they had selected. Over his arms, the sledge hammer lifted. Kirkpatrick shuddered. A blow of that terrific force would crush Martin's arm to a pulp! He saw the muscles knot and quiver in the naked back of the executioner as he tensed himself for an incredibly powerful blow!

Martin's eyes were closed. He strained away from the blow. He struggled, but the strength of the other two torturers was too much for him. His forearm was held immovably on the iron of the bar to which it was fastened—and the sledge hammer started downward!

The executioner who wielded the sledge hammer lifted on his toes. His back muscles galvanized in a completely coördinated effort. The sledge-hammer flashed downward with incredible speed, and as it moved it gained momentum. It was a titan's blow, and Kirkpatrick choked down a groan. It would be a miracle if that blow did not sever Martin's arm!

He heard the harsh clangor of the hammer striking steel, and a muffled shout. Martin had fallen backward across his chair...

Fallen backward? But how could he? With his wrists ironed to the railing, that would be impossible. Kirkpatrick's eyes flashed in bewilderment to the executioner who had struck the blow. He saw that the iron railing sagged to the floor, broken cleanly in half by that single incredible blow. And already the hammer was lifted again!

The other two executioners were staring at their hooded companion incredulously. Judge Torture's voice spoke harshly from the bench. And the man heaved the hammer a second time. His hands slipped from the handle of the heavy sledge, and it sailed through the air! It sailed with terrific speed, with unswerving aim—*straight at the head of Judge Torture!*

And through the chamber of horrors, there rang a curiously flat and metallic laughter, a mocking and ominous sound. It echoed with menace. It filled the room. And Kirkpatrick heard it without belief, and then he, too, laughed. He shouted.

*"The Spider!"* cried Kirkpatrick. *"The Spider has come!"* He shouted those words, and his voice broke with a sob!

EVEN AS he shouted, the hammer crunched home into the wigged and scarlet figure behind the bench. There was a sound of breaking wood, and the whole figure leaped into the air—sailed backward under the drive of that sledge! And now, for the first time, the Spider spoke!

"The bar is broken!" he hurled words at the men in the jury box. "Slide your shackles off the bar... *and attack!*"

As he spoke, he whipped off the black hood that had covered his head... and revealed the harsh and ruthless lines of the

Spider's face! A thin black silken cape fluttered down about his naked shoulders. Two guns leaped into his fists!

In the instant those guns struck his palms, they fired... and the two executioners were on the floor, twitching in their death-throes. But Kirkpatrick, even in this instant of wild jubilation, knew once more the touch of despair. For the tipstaffs of the six bailiffs were all focused upon the crouching, menacing figure of the Spider!

Kirkpatrick saw the strange power of those wands seize hold of the Spider, saw his muscles jerk and quiver into rigidity, even while he turned to bring those deadly guns to bear upon the men of Judge Torture! Not even the Spider could resist those mysterious weapons! Had they not held helpless twelve of the leading officials of the police? Had they not paralyzed Kirkpatrick, himself?

"Spider!" he shouted. "Spider, throw yourself to the floor! Break the spell of those wands!"

The Spider heard Kirkpatrick's shout as from a great distance. He was aware that the ten men whom he had freed with that single smashing blow of the hammer were immobilized by the fringes of the power focus of the six tipstaffs which were concentrated upon him. It was his battle, and his alone. If he could not break this strange power....

The twin guns in his fists were hot. They scorched his palms. His muscles had an iron rigidity that resisted all movement. And the six bailiffs, their faces pale, their wands thrust out toward him, were moving toward him slowly. Behind him, the voice of Judge Torture spoke dimly.

"Burn him down!" he ordered, and his voice blasted with harsh vibration. "Burn him down, fools!"

Wentworth felt the heat that tormented him increase sensibly. His jaw set like rock. His guns seemed frozen at his sides. They were aimed at nothing, could be aimed at nothing... unless he could break the power that could hold twelve men helpless!

Wentworth focused his eyes on one of the bailiffs, now a bare twenty feet away from him. He must kill that man. It was only necessary to shift the muzzle of his automatic six inches to the left and squeeze the trigger. That was all! Laughter pumped at Wentworth's chest, the laughter of the Spider! That was all... but it was more than the combined wills of twelve men had been able to accomplish!

WENTWORTH THREW his will into his right hand... and it was the will of the Master of Men! Veins squirmed, blue and contorted, in Wentworth's temples. Perspiration started out on his forehead. There were six red blots upon the naked flesh of his chest, six spots that were reddening into burns where the force of the tipstaffs struck him. His right hand was trembling. The muscles stood out like iron bands in his forearm. They turned blue with pressure. The cords of his fingers threatened to burst through the skin... and the gun had not moved even an inch!

Wentworth's breathing ceased. His chest swelled. His eyes bulged in their sockets. One of the bailiffs cried out in a strangled voice... and suddenly the Spider laughed!

His right hand had started to move!

It moved by fractions of an inch. His own muscles seemed to

fight against the movement. And it was not his strength which shifted that black muzzle with the slow inevitability of a glacier's flow to the sea. It was his will, the impregnable, irresistible will of the Master of Men!

The bailiff at the right of the encroaching semi-circle began to tremble. His lips squirmed back from his teeth.

"No!" he gasped. *"No!"*

But even as he squeezed out the words, the aim of the tipstaffs was shifting, was lifting! In an instant, the tension of his arm broke, and the tipstaff whipped upward and focused on his own face! The man shouted... and the Spider's gun slashed fire and death across the courtroom of Judge Torture!

Once more the Spider laughed. "Fools!" he whispered. "Fools! Do you think you can conquer... the Master of Men!"

Once more, the death of the Spider's guns struck in that room, and another of the bailiffs was flung backward in sudden, bloody death! It was as if the Spider had pronounced a talisman against harm. In that same instant, the morale of the bailiffs broke. Their unconquerable weapons had been beaten by the will of one man—at what terrible cost, even they did not realize.

The four bailiffs who remained dropped their wands and turned to flee, and there was a brief, sustained roar of gunfire. Four shots sped unerringly from the twin guns of the Spider— and four men sprawled, dying, upon the floor!

The last of Judge Torture's men was down and the Spider swayed in his tracks, sagged weakly against an upright of the shattered iron bar which had held the jurors as prisoners! His head seemed too heavy for the powerful column of his neck. On his chest burned the medallions of the tipstaff torment. His eyes, shadowed by the bushy black brows of the Spider, sought out Kirkpatrick, where he stood, still chained, in the prisoner's dock.

"I was too late to save Carstairs," he said slowly. "It took a while to find out which of the grain elevators about the city used trucks thirty-two feet long."

He pushed himself away from the iron railing, and it was only his will which kept his tormented body in motion. He went past the bodies of the torturers toward the bench of Judge Torture.

"A few seconds after I located this barge and entered, the executioner came out through the curtains," he said. "I took his place. But in order to save you and your men, I have had to let Judge Torture himself escape."

HE WAS beside the bench now, and Kirkpatrick found his voice. "Nonsense, man," he said sharply. "You smashed him to a pulp with that sledge hammer! We have to thank you... for our lives, Spider! The city owes you... the lives of many of its citizens!"

Wentworth was bending over. He whipped up the scarlet robe of Judge Torture, the white wig and tossed them across the bench.

"Judge Torture escaped," he said. "I did this only to break the courage of his men. This is a dummy. Torture spoke through a microphone. Judge Torture himself might have been any man in this room!"

As he bent over the bench, resting his weight, relaxing the strain that racked all his body, a voice cut harshly across the courtroom of Judge Torture.

"Up with your hands, Spider!" it commanded with bitter force. "I arrest you for murder!"

Kirkpatrick's head swung about. Inspector Littlejohn held a gun in his still-shackled hands, a gun filched from the body of a dead bailiff, and it was leveled directly at the Spider! Protest leaped to Kirkpatrick's lips, and he choked it back. Ungrateful though it seemed, this was just. The Spider was wanted for a hundred crimes. It was for the courts, not the police, to show mercy! So Kirkpatrick reasoned, but his face was pale with anger and his eyes blazed at Littlejohn.

The Spider laughed softly. "My dear inspector!" came his mocking, metallic voice. "I compliment you upon your singleness of purpose! It could almost be termed a virtue! I am sorry I cannot permit you to arrest me! Kirkpatrick, your men are on the way here. Sergeant Reams received orders from Wentworth, and I was fortunate enough to be before them."

"Up with your hands, Spider!" Littlejohn snapped. "Or I'll shoot you!"

The Spider nodded equably, lifted both hands above his head. "I could kill you easily, Littlejohn," he said, "thanks to the forethought of Judge Torture. An ingenious man, this Torture. He also provided... a way of escape!"

As Wentworth paused in his speech, the room was suddenly in darkness... as it had been before the entrance of Judge Torture. Littlejohn's gun crashed flame across the blackness. His curses lifted frenziedly... Then the lights blinked on again. The scarlet robe of Judge Torture had vanished from the bench.

The laughter of the Spider seemed to whisper into the court-room. But the Spider himself... had vanished!

## CHAPTER 10
## DEATH TO THE SPIDER!

LITTLEJOHN DASHED furiously to the trapdoor through which Wentworth had dropped, and which Judge Torture had provided for the quick disappearance of the dummy in emergency. He pounded at the trapdoor, found and manipulated a lever, but the opening remained stubbornly closed.

The other officers were beginning to stir wearily, freed at last from the power of the tipstaffs. Kirkpatrick lifted his voice in sharp orders and presently, freed, he was able to lead his associates toward the shore. Behind them, as they left the courtroom, there was a sudden muffled blast... and hot flames leaped up! It was instantly followed by a series of other small blasts, as the abandoned tipstaffs burst into flame.

Kirkpatrick hurried his men ahead of him. Inspector Little-john walked stiffly at a distance, for there was hostility in the eyes of the other men who looked toward him. They had been saved from incredibly horrid death by the Spider... and yet Littlejohn had tried to arrest him! Kirkpatrick was frowning over what the Spider had said just before Littlejohn's challenge.

"Judge Torture spoke over a microphone! He might have been *any man in this room!*"

And Kirkpatrick realized it was true. In the concentration upon the horrors of torture, no man would have noticed whether

144

his neighbor was secretly speaking into a microphone. It is a curious fact that when identical simultaneous sound comes from two different points at once, it is impossible to detect the source of the sound! And Judge Torture spoke always in a whisper....

Kirkpatrick's eyes went to Littlejohn. No, he could not believe these horrors of Inspector Littlejohn.

They were on the deck of the barge now, and flames were beginning to poke red tongues up through the cracks in the deck. From the shore came a hail.

"Commissioner!" it called. "Are you all right?"

"All right, Sergeant Reams!" Kirkpatrick called back, recognizing the voice. "Throw guards along the shore here, and allow no one to escape!"

"Already done, sir!" Sergeant Reams called. "Mr. Wentworth gave orders, sir."

Kirkpatrick frowned as he found the gangplank. There was in his brain an unshakable conviction that Wentworth and the Spider were one man. But how could the Spider be on board the barge, and Wentworth ashore, if that were the case?

HE STEPPED ashore and, from the shadows, Richard Wentworth moved forward to greet him.

"I'm sorry to have interfered, Kirkpatrick," he said shortly, "since you ordered me to withdraw from the case. However, I believed your life was in danger. I perceive that I was wrong."

Kirkpatrick stared fixedly at Wentworth, standing so erectly, his eyes challenging. He said slowly, "I was in danger, Dick, but the Spider saved me. Have you been ashore long?"

145

146

# JUDGEMENT OF THE DAMNED

Wentworth shrugged irritably. "Ask Sergeant Reams," he said shortly. "Since you are safe, I will withdraw once more!"

Littlejohn's voice rang out harshly. "Just a moment, Wentworth!" he said. "I want to take a look at your chest!"

Sergeant Reams pushed into the little circle about the foot of the gangplank. "Mr. Wentworth has been keeping watch here, with the rest of us, sir," he said.

Wentworth laughed sharply. "It seems, Kirkpatrick, that I am more of a burden than a help. Is it still necessary for Inspector Littlejohn to… take a look at my chest?"

Kirkpatrick waved a hand impatiently. "No, Dick, of course not," he said quietly.

Wentworth clicked his heels in a sharp bow, and strode off across the grain elevator yard toward where he had parked his car. He heard Littlejohn's voice rasping, and lengthened his stride. They would find out soon enough that he had preceded Sergeant Reams to the yard, and met him at the gate… and from darkness. That had been necessary since he was dripping wet from his plunge through Judge's Torture's trapdoor into the North River.

He had sent Sergeant Reams and the others to the river-bank while he himself made a hurried change in his car. It had been a narrow escape. That was a minor matter. What was important now was that Judge Torture had escaped, and that he must be brought to justice!

Only once in his wild race southward along the river did Wentworth pause, and then it was to resume the identity of the Spider!

## JUDGEMENT OF THE DAMNED

CITY HALL PARK was crowded with thousands of persons who had attended Morris Bacon's torchlight parade and mass meeting against the Spider. There were police on the outskirts of the crowd, but they stood idly for the most part, hands clasped behind them.

Above the heads of the crowd burned torches of red fire. A man had climbed up the base of the statue of Civic Virtue and was haranguing the people... shouting that the Spider had killed people by torture, as proved by the seals upon the foreheads of the dead! The Spider must be destroyed.

The speaker was young and convincing.

"The Spider murdered my dad!" he said. "I came here to exact vengeance! I have seen the Spider face to face, and warned him that I will shoot him on sight! Had I known then, what I know now, I would not have warned him! I would have killed him then and there!"

The crowd roared its approval of Jack Murdock, and he went on shouting at the people, exhorting them. He told them the police must be forced to strike against the Spider. "They must know who he is!" he cried. "For years, he has had his own way in this city. He has struck, and killed, and no man has stopped him! People of New York, *we* must stop him! I will tell you how!"

He paused then, and a tense waiting silence fell over the crowd. Into that silence, a shrieking whine broke—the scream of dry-skidding tires. A few heads turned aside from the speaker to stare toward Broadway. A coupé was rocketing out of the side street.

The coupé darted straight across the street, hurdled the curb and skimmed past a statue. It crashed into a fence, shuddered to a halt. The doors punched open, and a man staggered to the ground. The man's shoulders were crooked, and his stride was a limp. From his shoulders hung a heel-length black cape, and a broad-brimmed black hat was dragged low over his eyes.

A whisper murmured through the crowd, a whisper that began a roar. And that roar was a single word:

"*Spider!*"

A half block away, braced against the statue of Civic Virtue, Jack Murdock stared out over the crowd and his face went pale. He lifted a clenched fist above his head.

"There he is!" he shouted. "There's the Spider! Kill him! *Death to the Spider!*"

Then the Spider turned and ran!

THE SPIDER'S pace seemed uncertain. He reeled in his running, and the billowing folds of the cape seemed too much for him to manage. A gun cracked out somewhere on the outskirts of the crowd. The uniformed police were thrusting forward. But the Spider did not dart toward his car. He ran toward the City Hall!

There were police at guard before the big bronze doors. He swerved aside from that, leaped high toward a window. The glass shattered as he swung himself to the sill… shattered under the impact of bullets fired from the crowd!

Then the Spider leaped over the sill and vanished into the interior of the City Hall! Moments later, the mob poured up the steps of the building. The police tried to turn them aside. They were overwhelmed in an instant.

Then suddenly, the mob that flowed back over the pavement of the park fell silent. They were all staring up at the capital frieze above the door, the ledge which was sheltered beneath the wide overhang of the roof. The Spider stood there!

That silence lasted for a moment only, and then the shouts lifted higher than ever. Guns blasted out in the crowd, and stone dust flew in white puffs of fury from the masonry at the Spider's feet, from the white columns that flanked him.

Then a man began to fight his way forward through the crowd. His hands were lifted high above his head.

"Hold your fire!" he cried. "The Spider cannot escape us! We will fill the building with armed men! We will execute him!"

Faces turned toward him, and the crowd respectfully made way. This was their leader. This was the man whose brother had been slain by Judge Torture… by the Spider, and who had a right to vengeance. By his side marched Jack Murdock, his face white, gun in his fist.

Murdock thrust a violent way through the mob, opening a path for Morris Bacon. He struck out about him; he cried hoarsely. Over on the edge of the park, a police riot car jerked to a halt. The cops plunged into the crowd, except for one man who stood rigidly erect upon the truck. He had a rifle in his hand, and his narrow face was grimly set. Inspector Littlejohn.

Littlejohn swore and leaped to the ground with the rifle in his hand. He was not in uniform. The crowd opened to let through a man with a weapon that might bring down the Spider!

Morris Bacon was strangely silent as he moved forward

toward the steps of the City Hall. He moved with a curious stiffness, with a hard tension of all his muscles.

Ahead of him, Jack Murdock cried out. "Way! Way for the avenger! For the man whose brother was killed by the Spider! Whose daughter was tortured by the Spider! Whose hand is crippled by the torture of the Spider!"

MORRIS BACON did not seem to want to go forward. He was struggling, as if with himself. He braced his legs stiffly, but he moved forward. He was at the bottom step now. He was mounting beside Jack Murdock. Inspector Littlejohn leaped to the steps, the rifle ready in his fist. He braced and threw the gun to his shoulder, aiming straight up at the figure of the Spider!

Abruptly, a startled cry lifted from the mob. Something snake-like and thin looped down from that ledge where the Spider stood! Though no man had seen that figure move, there was no mistaking what that snake-like thing was! It was the Spider's web!

Even as they cried out, the noose of the web settled about the shoulders of one of the men upon the steps of City Hall. And that man rose into the air! He lifted straight upward! He was struggling, fighting madly against the silken web which bit deeply into his arms, but he went upward nonetheless!

The mob saw the man dragged over the edge of the ledge. He leaped to his feet and hurled himself at the becaped figure. There was a flurry of the swirling cape, angry shouts, and the two struggling figures plunged back into the darkness behind the columns, under the shadow of the roof.

The mob went mad in those waiting moments. Men beat

once more at the bronze doors. Others leaped to the windows and crashed through the glass. And then… and then two figures staggered out into sight again upon the ledge. One of those men was on his feet. He held the other high above his head, gripped in two powerful hands… and it was the man in the robes of the Spider who was held thus helplessly high above the head of his conqueror!

For a long moment, the two figures poised there, high above the heads of the mob. Then a voice rang out clearly.

"Death!" it cried. *"Death to the Spider!"*

The figure in the Spider's robes plummeted downward through space! It fell upon the steps of the City Hall, and in an instant, the mob closed in upon it! Feet trampled upon the prostrate body. A man wielded a cobblestone like a club. Hands and feet tore and beat upon the man in the robes of the Spider.

There was no one to hold back the few police who remained on their feet now. They moved forward through the crowd, hut they moved slowly.

When they reached there presently, the mob had done its work. What lay upon the steps of City Hall could not be called human. It was a shattered pulp, a broken bag of flesh and blood.

"All right now!" called the cop. "All right now. Give way. One side!"

The mob stared down at its bloody work, its anger suddenly sated. They were men again, and they looked at their hands which had done this thing, and at their stained shoes, and they were frightened. They shrank back… and it was only then that it became apparent that a beam of light had played down upon their backs while they performed their slaughter—a beam of light from a hand torch that dangled over the edge of the ledge.

As they stepped back, the finger of brilliance performed a slow circle on the sidewalk. It was focused to a bright round spot, and that spot slid slowly over the steps. It crossed the body of the thing that had been human and passed on. It came back again to that body and remained focused there. It was a round, bright spot of light, but there was a shadow in its heart.

The shadow of... *the Spider's seal!*

A man sobbed out a curse as that shadow of sprawled hairy legs and poison fangs ceased to whirl and focused on the dead man. And it seemed that in the waiting silence, there was a soft and mocking laughter, a metallic laughter... the laughter of the Spider!

There was no mistaking the fact that words came from the high air, seemingly from a great distance.

*"Judge Torture... is dead!"*

AMONG THE crowd, one man had shrunk back from the bloody slaughter. This was not his sort of work. He could face a man with a gun in his fist, but this... this *slaughter*.

He shrank back, and looked up toward the place where the Spider and his captive had fought, and he was gazing there when he heard the laughter and the pronouncement of doom. His eyes were quick. They could penetrate the shadow where others, shaken by their own terror, could not see. He saw that there were two parallel wires that stretched away from the roof of the City Hall—and that those wires sagged more than was normal!

His eyes followed the course of the wires and he began to push away through the crowd.

He reached the statue of Nathan Hale, where it stood with its background of trees. He was there, when the man dropped to earth and stepped into the shadows of the statue.

He said, "Gee, that was great work, Mr. Bacon! If anybody had a better right than Jack Murdock to kill the Spider, it was you!"

The man in the shadow of the statue stiffened at the unexpected voice. He turned his head slowly. He said, "Did you notice the left hand of the man... who fell to the steps?"

"The—the left hand?"

"Yes, the left hand," said the man. "It was badly wounded. It was crippled... by being pierced by a meat hook!"

Jack Murdock gasped. He fell back a step. "Good Lord!" he stammered. "You mean it was—Mr. Bacon in the Spider's *robes?* You mean the Spider dragged him up there, put his robes on him, and threw Mr. Bacon down to the mob! You mean that *you're*—" Jack Murdock's hand whipped up and it pointed a revolver. "All right, Spider!" he said harshly! "I've got you now! Go for your gun!"

In the shadows, the man laughed and stepped slowly out into the light. It was the Spider, cape and hat gone, his shoulders straight, but still with the stern and bitter face of the Spider.

"A moment, Murdock," he said quietly. "You heard me say... *Judge Torture is dead!*"

Murdock said harshly, "Go for your gun!"

Wentworth shook his head, "Shoot, if you like, but I wish you

155

would wait a moment, while I speak. While I show you what I have in my car. It is only a few steps away. Yes, I said Judge Torture is dead. Judge Torture, a man who delighted in tormenting his fellow men to death; who destroyed his own brother because that brother knew of his sadistic tendencies and might suspect who was behind the deeds of Judge Torture. A man who deliberately set about clearing himself by inflicting a terrible wound in his hand... no doubt carefully cocained beforehand. Who planned that scene before captives whom he planned to release afterward so that he would have witnesses to clear him. I don't think that he intended to kill his daughter at that time. I think he intended to get free and kill his torturers before they could harm her. But I beat him to it."

Murdock said slowly, "You're crazy! You're trying to lie out of this! Why, I saw Judge Torture... and Mr. Bacon at the same time!"

WENTWORTH SHOOK his head. "You saw a dummy of Judge Torture. You heard Bacon speaking over a microphone. Here is my car... and here, Murdock, is the proof that Judge Torture and Morris Bacon were one and the same man!"

Wentworth gestured toward the seat of his car. Spread there was the robe of Judge Torture, of crimson silk. Beside it was a torn scrap of the same silk.

"Look, Murdock," Wentworth whispered. "You know where that scrap of silk came from. It was torn from Anne Bacon's dress. You heard her say that she liked the silk so well that *she bought up the entire batch of that particular cloth!*"

Murdock said, "I remember, but—"

## JUDGEMENT OF THE DAMNED

"You know that no two dyeings of cloth, no matter how closely the formula is matched, are ever exactly the same!" Wentworth said. "But the silk of Judge Torture's robe, and the silk of Anne Bacon's dress… are identical! No one else but Anne's father could have had access to that silk. No—one else would have used it.

"Judge Torture is Morris Bacon!" Wentworth whispered. "Judge Torture—is dead!"

Jack Murdock stared at the silk. He shook his head, and his fists knotted at his side. "You are right," he said thickly. "You have to be right… I'm beginning to understand now. You put your seal on those victims of Judge Torture to hold down the terror he wanted to create. You—you have saved the people of the city from a terrible tyranny. And you didn't mind that they blamed you for it."

Jack Murdock drew in a shuddering breath. "You killed my father. You killed the father of the girl I love. Morris Bacon deserved death. My father… I can't say but one thing, Spider. My… my vengeance doesn't mean a thing. I don't know why you killed my father, but I do know one thing. I—I have no right to take vengeance, when it would deprive the world of so great a man as you!"

Jack Murdock's head came up slowly. He stared before him across the seat where the silk lay spread, and his eyes were blurred.

"Spider, let me—let me serve with you!"

He turned to face the Spider, and a sharp cry escaped his lips. The Spider… had vanished.

## THE SPIDER

| | |
|---|---|
| ❑ #1: The Spider Strikes | $13.95 |
| ❑ #2: The Wheel of Death | $13.95 |
| ❑ #3: Wings of the Black Death | $13.95 |
| ❑ #4: City of Flaming Shadows | $13.95 |
| ❑ #5: Empire of Doom! | $13.95 |
| ❑ #6: Citadel of Hell | $13.95 |
| ❑ #7: The Serpent of Destruction | $13.95 |
| ❑ #8: The Mad Horde | $13.95 |
| ❑ #9: Satan's Death Blast | $13.95 |
| ❑ #10: The Corpse Cargo | $13.95 |
| ❑ #11: Prince of the Red Looters | $13.95 |
| ❑ #12: Reign of the Silver Terror | $13.95 |
| ❑ #13: Builders of the Dark Empire | $13.95 |
| ❑ #14: Death's Crimson Juggernaut | $13.95 |
| ❑ #15: The Red Death Rain | $13.95 |
| ❑ #16: The City Destroyer | $13.95 |
| ❑ #17: The Pain Emperor | $13.95 |
| ❑ #18: The Flame Master | $13.95 |
| ❑ #19: Slaves of the Crime Master | $13.95 |
| ❑ #20: Reign of the Death Fiddler | $13.95 |
| ❑ #21: Hordes of the Red Butcher | $13.95 |
| ❑ #22: Dragon Lord of the Underworld | $13.95 |
| ❑ #23: Master of the Death-Madness | $13.95 |
| ❑ #24: King of the Red Killers | $13.95 |
| ❑ #25: Overlord of the Damned | $13.95 |
| ❑ #26: Death Reign of the Vampire King | $13.95 |
| ❑ #27: Emperor of the Yellow Death | $13.95 |
| ❑ #28: The Mayor of Hell | $13.95 |
| ❑ #29: Slaves of the Murder Syndicate | $13.95 |
| ❑ #30: Green Globes of Death | $13.95 |
| ❑ #31: The Cholera King | $13.95 |
| ❑ #32: Slaves of the Dragon | $13.95 |
| ❑ #33: Legions of Madness | $12.95 |
| ❑ #34: Laboratory of the Damned | $12.95 |
| ❑ #35: Satan's Sightless Legion | $12.95 |
| ❑ #36: The Coming of the Terror | $12.95 |
| ❑ #37: The Devil's Death-Dwarfs | $12.95 |
| ❑ #38: City of Dreadful Night | $12.95 |
| ❑ #39: Reign of the Snake Men | $12.95 |
| ❑ #40: Dictator of the Damned | $12.95 |
| ❑ #41: The Mill-Town Massacres | $12.95 |
| ❑ #42: Satan's Workshop | $12.95 |
| ❑ #43: Scourge of the Yellow Fangs | $12.95 |
| ❑ #44: The Devil's Pawnbroker | $12.95 |
| ❑ #45: Voyage of the Coffin Ship | $12.95 |
| ❑ #46: The Man Who Ruled in Hell | $13.95 |
| ❑ #47: Slaves of the Black Monarch | $13.95 |
| ❑ #48: Machineguns Over the White House | $13.95 |
| ❑ #49: The City That Dared Not Eat | $13.95 |
| ❑ #50: Master of the Flaming Horde | $13.95 |
| ❑ #51: Satan's Switchboard | $13.95 |
| ❑ #52: Legions of the Accursed Light | $13.95 |
| ❑ #53: The City of Lost Men | $13.95 |
| ❑ #54: The Grey Horde Creeps | $13.95 |

| | |
|---|---|
| ❑ #55: City of Whispering Death | $13.95 |
| ❑ #56: When Thousands Slept in Hell | $13.95 |
| ❑ #57: Satan's Shakles | $14.95 |
| ❑ #58: The Emperor From Hell | $14.95 |
| ❑ #59: The Devil's Candlesticks | $14.95 |
| ❑ #60: The City That Paid to Die | $14.95 |
| ❑ #61: The Spider at Bay | $14.95 |
| ❑ #62: Scourge of the Black Legions | $14.95 |
| ❑ #63: The Withering Death | $14.95 |
| ❑ #64: Claws of the Golden Dragon | $14.95 |
| ❑ #65: The Song of Death | $14.95 |
| ❑ #66: The Silver Death Reign | $14.95 |
| ❑ #67: Blight of the Blazing Eye | $14.95 |
| ❑ #68: King of the Fleshless Legion | $14.95 |
| ❑ #69: Rule of the Monster Men | $16.95 |
| ❑ #70: The Spider and the Slaves of Hell | $16.95 |
| ❑ #71: The Spider and the Fire God | $16.95 |
| ❑ #72: The Corpse Broker | $16.95 |
| ❑ #73: The Spider and the Eyeless Legion | $16.95 |
| ❑ #74: The Spider and the Faceless One | $16.95 |
| ❑ #75: Satan's Murder Machines | $16.95 |
| ❑ #76: The Spider and the Pain Master | $16.95 |
| ❑ #77: Hell's Sales Manager | $16.95 |
| ❑ #78: Slaves of the Laughing Death | $16.95 |
| ❑ #79: The Man From Hell | $16.95 |
| ❑ #80: The Spider and the War Emperor | $16.95 |
| ❑ *NEW:* #81: Judgement of the Damned | $17.95 |

## THE WESTERN RAIDER

| | |
|---|---|
| ❑ #1: Guns of the Damned | $13.95 |
| ❑ #2: The Hawk Rides Back from Death | $13.95 |
| ❑ #3: Gun-Call for the Lost Legion | $13.95 |
| ❑ #4: The Law of Silver Trent | $13.95 |
| ❑ #5: The Gun-Prayer of Silver Trent | $13.95 |
| ❑ #6: Silver Trent Rides Alone | $13.95 |

## CAPTAIN SATAN

| | |
|---|---|
| ❑ #1: The Mask of the Damned | $13.95 |
| ❑ #2: Parole for the Dead | $13.95 |
| ❑ #3: The Dead Man Express | $13.95 |
| ❑ #4: A Ghost Rides the Dawn | $13.95 |
| ❑ #5: The Ambassador From Hell | $13.95 |

## DR. YEN SIN

| | |
|---|---|
| ❑ #1: Mystery of the Dragon's Shadow | $12.95 |
| ❑ #2: Mystery of the Golden Skull | $12.95 |
| ❑ #3: Mystery of the Singing Mummies | $12.95 |

## THE MASKED MARKSMAN

| | |
|---|---|
| ❑ #1: Death Takes an Encore | $16.95 |
| ❑ #2: Death's Understudy | $16.95 |
| ❑ #3: Death Steals the Act | $16.95 |
| ❑ #4: Top Billing for Murder | $16.95 |

# POPULAR HERO PULPS  AVAILABLE NOW:

## OPERATOR 5
- ❏ #1: The Masked Invasion — $13.95
- ❏ #2: The Invisible Empire — $13.95
- ❏ #3: The Yellow Scourge — $13.95
- ❏ #4: The Melting Death — $13.95
- ❏ #5: Cavern of the Damned — $13.95
- ❏ #6: Master of Broken Men — $13.95
- ❏ #7: Invasion of the Dark Legions — $13.95
- ❏ #8: The Green Death Mists — $13.95
- ❏ #9: Legions of Starvation — $13.95
- ❏ #10: The Red Invader — $13.95
- ❏ #11: The League of War-Monsters — $13.95
- ❏ #12: The Army of the Dead — $13.95
- ❏ #13: March of the Flame Marauders — $13.95
- ❏ #14: Blood Reign of the Dictator — $13.95
- ❏ #15: Invasion of the Yellow Warlords — $13.95
- ❏ #16: Legions of the Death Master — $13.95
- ❏ #17: Hosts of the Flaming Death — $13.95
- ❏ #18: Invasion of the Crimson Death Cult — $13.95
- ❏ #19: Attack of the Blizzard Men — $13.95
- ❏ #20: Scourge of the Invisible Death — $13.95
- ❏ #21: Raiders of the Red Death — $13.95
- ❏ #22: War-Dogs of the Green Destroyer — $13.95
- ❏ #23: Rockets From Hell — $13.95
- ❏ #24: War-Masters from the Orient — $13.95
- ❏ #25: Crime's Reign of Terror — $13.95
- ❏ #26: Death's Ragged Army — $13.95
- ❏ #27: Patriots' Death Battalion — $13.95
- ❏ #28: The Bloody Forty-five Days — $13.95
- ❏ #29: America's Plague Battalions — $13.95
- ❏ #30: Liberty's Suicide Legions — $13.95
- ❏ #31: Siege of the Thousand Patriots — $13.95
- ❏ #32: Patriots' Death March — $14.95
- ❏ #33: Revolt of the Lost Legions — $14.95
- ❏ #34: Drums of Destruction — $14.95
- ❏ #35: The Army Without a Country — $14.95
- ❏ #36: The Bloody Frontiers — $14.95
- ❏ #37: The Coming of the Mongol Hordes — $14.95
- ❏ #38: The Siege That Brought Black Death — $16.95
- ❏ #39: Revolt of the Devil Men — $16.95
- ❏ #40: The Suicide Battalion — $16.95
- ❏ #41: The Day of the Damned — $16.95
- ❏ #42: The Dawn That Shook the World — $16.95
- ❏ #43: When Hell Came to America — $16.95
- ❏ #44: Invasion From the Sky — $16.95
- ❏ *NEW:* #45: The Winged Horror of the Yellow Vulture — $17.95

## G-8 AND HIS BATTLE ACES
- ❏ #1: The Bat Staffel — $13.95

## CAPTAIN COMBAT
- ❏ #1: The Sky Beast of Berlin — $13.95
- ❏ #2: Red Wings For the Blood Battalion — $13.95
- ❏ #3: Low Ceiling For Nazi Hell Hawks — $13.95

## ACE G-MAN
- ❏ #1: The Suicide Squad Reports for Death — $14.95
- ❏ #2: Coffins for the Suicide Squad — $14.95
- ❏ #3: Shells for the Suicide Squad — $14.95
- ❏ #4: The Suicide Squad in Corpse-Town — $14.95
- ❏ #5: Wanted–In Three Pine Coffins — $14.95
- ❏ #6: The Suicide Squad's Dawn Patrol — $14.95
- ❏ #7: Targets for the Flaming Arrow — $16.95

## DUSTY AYRES AND HIS BATTLE BIRDS
- ❏ #1: Black Lightning! — $13.95
- ❏ #2: Crimson Doom — $13.95
- ❏ #3: The Purple Tornado — $13.95
- ❏ #4: The Screaming Eye — $13.95
- ❏ #5: The Green Thunderbolt — $13.95
- ❏ #6: The Red Destroyer — $13.95
- ❏ #7: The White Death — $13.95
- ❏ #8: The Black Avenger — $13.95
- ❏ #9: The Silver Typhoon — $13.95
- ❏ #10: The Troposphere F-S — $13.95
- ❏ #11: The Blue Cyclone — $13.95
- ❏ #12: The Tesla Raiders — $13.95

## MAVERICKS
- ❏ #1: Five Against the Law — $12.95
- ❏ #2: Mesquite Manhunters — $12.95
- ❏ #3: Bait for the Lobo Pack — $12.95
- ❏ #4: Doc Grimson's Outlaw Posse — $12.95
- ❏ #5: Charlie Parr's Gunsmoke Cure — $12.95

## THE MYSTERIOUS WU FANG
- ❏ #1: The Case of the Six Coffins — $12.95
- ❏ #2: The Case of the Scarlet Feather — $12.95
- ❏ #3: The Case of the Yellow Mask — $12.95
- ❏ #4: The Case of the Suicide Tomb — $12.95
- ❏ #5: The Case of the Green Death — $12.95
- ❏ #6: The Case of the Black Lotus — $12.95
- ❏ #7: The Case of the Hidden Scourge — $12.95

## THE SECRET 6
- ❏ #1: The Red Shadow — $13.95
- ❏ #2: House of Walking Corpses — $13.95
- ❏ #3: The Monster Murders — $13.95
- ❏ #4: The Golden Alligator — $13.95

## CAPTAIN ZERO
- ❏ #1: City of Deadly Sleep — $13.95
- ❏ #2: The Mark of Zero! — $13.95
- ❏ #3: The Golden Murder Syndicate — $13.95

## RED FINGER
- ❏ #1: Second-Hand Death — $24.95

www.ingramcontent.com/pod-product-compliance
Lightning Source LLC
Chambersburg PA
CBHW051136260626
47170CB00005B/1835